Praise for the

"Daley's characters come ~~filled~~ filled with a little mystery and a little romance which makes ___ a murderous adventure."

– Tonya Kappes,
USA Today Bestselling Author of *Fixin' To Die*

"Daley's mysteries offer as much sizzle and pop as fireworks on a hot summer's day."

– Mary Kennedy,
Author of The Dream Club Mysteries

"I'm a huge fan of Kathi's books. I think I've read every one. Without a doubt, she's a ˙gifted cozy mystery author and I eagerly await each new release!"

– Dianne Harman,
Author of the High Desert Cozy Mysteries

"Intriguing, likeable characters, keep-you-guessing mysteries, and settings that literally transport you to Paradise...Daley's stories draw you in and keep you glued until the very last page."

– Tracy Weber,
Agatha-Nominated Author of the Downward Dog Mysteries

"Daley really knows how to write a top-notch cozy."

– *MJB Reviewers*

"Kathi Daley writes a story with a puzzling cold-case mystery while highlighting...the love of home, family, and good friends."

– *Chatting About Cozies*

Beaches

A TJ JENSEN MYSTERY

IN

PARADISE

**The Tj Jensen Mystery Series
by Kathi Daley**

PUMPKINS IN PARADISE (#1)
SNOWMEN IN PARADISE (#2)
BIKINIS IN PARADISE (#3)
CHRISTMAS IN PARADISE (#4)
PUPPIES IN PARADISE (#5)
HALLOWEEN IN PARADISE (#6)
TREASURE IN PARADISE (#7)
FIREWORKS IN PARADISE (#8)
BEACHES IN PARADISE (#9)

Beaches

A TJ JENSEN MYSTERY

IN PARADISE

KATHI DALEY

HENERY PRESS

Copyright

BEAHCES IN PARADISE
A Tj Jensen Mystery
Part of the Henery Press Mystery Collection

First Edition | July 2018

Henery Press, LLC
www.henerypress.com

Trade Paperback ISBN-13: 978-1-63511-380-8
Digital epub ISBN-13: 978-1-63511-381-5
Kindle ISBN-13: 978-1-63511-382-2
Hardcover ISBN-13: 978-1-63511-383-9

Printed in the United States of America

*This beachy book is dedicated to
my beach loving "daughter" Brennen Amber Daley,
the best wife, mother, and friend, my son could ever
have prayed for and I could ever have hoped for.
Love you B.*

ACKNOWLEDGMENTS

They say it takes a village and I have a great one.

I want to thank all my friends who hang out over at my Kathi Daley Books Group page on Facebook. This exceptional group help me not only with promotion, but also with helpful suggestion and feedback as well.

I want to thank the bloggers and reviewers who have pretty much adopted me and have helped me to build a fantastic social media presence. There are too many to list, but I want to specifically recognize Mary Brown from *MJB Reviewers*.

I want to thank my fellow authors who I run to all the time when I don't know how to do something or how to deal with a situation. I have to say that the cozy mystery family is about as close knit a family as you are likely to find anywhere.

I want to thank my book club moderator Jayme Maness for the hours of fun, Bruce Curran for generously helping me with all my techy questions, Jessica Fisher for help with my ads and graphics, and Peggy Hyndman for help sleuthing out those pesky typos.

I want to thank Randy Ladenheim-Gil for making what I write legible.

I want to thank Art Molinares for welcoming me so enthusiastically to the Henery Press family, and a special thank you to the entire editing crew who have been so incredibly awesome and fun to work with.

And last but certainly not least, I want to thank my super-husband Ken for allowing me time to write by taking care of everything else (and I mean everything.)

CHAPTER 1

Thursday, August 10

The flickering glow of color produced by the bonfire on the beach created an eerie reflection on the still water of nearby Paradise Lake. The warm daytime temperature had cooled considerably once the sun set behind the distant mountain. I'd pulled on a sweatshirt but still felt chilled as I moved away from the warm flames toward the shadows, where I could be alone with my thoughts. My best friend, Jenna Elston, had taken my two half-sisters, Ashley and Gracie, camping, which meant my boyfriend, Kyle Donovan, and I had the entire weekend all to ourselves.

Finally.

Kyle and I had been friends for almost four years but had only become romantically involved in the past six weeks. We'd shared our first kiss in June but hadn't really had a chance to explore our relationship before a few weeks ago. Tonight would be the night we'd take our relationship to the next level. An intimate level. A level I knew would change everything. I couldn't remember when I'd been so happy *and* so nervous.

"So, Tj Jensen, what has you so enthralled that you're standing all the way over here by yourself?" asked Kyle as he walked up behind me and placed his arms around my waist.

I glanced at the others gathered around the bonfire for the kick off to the school year gathering Serenity High School sponsored each year for the staff. While the group appeared to be having a good time, I had other things on my mind. "I was thinking about us and our weekend together. It's been hard to wait for the right time, but now that it's here, I'm glad we decided not to rush things." I leaned into Kyle's body and let his warmth melt the tension from the day. It had been a busy week at Maggie's Hideaway, the lakeside resort where I lived and worked part-time when my dad's away. Not only was my dad in Sacramento, meeting with the physical therapist who would help him through his recovery from the auto accident he'd been involved in at the end of June, but this weekend was Summer Festival at Paradise Lake, so I'd been going nonstop all week. I supposed only those involved in the tourist industry could really understand the amount of effort it took to get everything ready for the throngs of visitors who were expected to make the trip up the mountain from the larger cities in the valley below.

"I've been thinking about the weekend as well." Kyle kissed my neck. "Quite a lot, to be honest. In some ways I feel like I've been waiting for this my whole life."

"We've only been together for a little over a month," I reminded Kyle as chills worked their way from my neck down my spine.

"Maybe. But I think I knew this was where we were heading from the moment I met you."

I smiled and stared at the dark horizon as I replayed the

memory of our first meeting in my mind. I remember the butterflies in my stomach as I struck up a conversation with the handsomest man I'd ever seen. I'd tried reminding myself that he was a guest and therefore completely off limits, but even in those first moments of conversation, I'd known Kyle would play an important part in my life.

"Do you have the whole weekend off?" Kyle asked.

"No," I answered regretfully. "But I have most of it. The staff decided to cut back on the number of Summer Festival events we're hosting this year because my dad's laid up. I volunteered for a few of the events in town, but I don't have anything tomorrow and the only ones I'll need to help out with at the resort are on Saturday evening."

Kyle kissed my neck. "So, until then?"

"I'm totally, blissfully free."

Kyle tightened his arms around my waist and pulled me back against him. I leaned my head against his chest and gazed out over the large freshwater lake as the moon peeked from behind the distant mountain peak. "Did you see that?" I asked as my eyes focused in on a flash of light across the inky black water.

"See what?" Kyle answered, still nuzzling my neck.

I raised my arm and pointed, desperately trying to distract myself from the sensation created by Kyle's lips as they dipped toward my collarbone. "I saw a light across the lake. I think it was coming from Rosenberg Island."

Kyle lifted his head, which allowed my heart rate to slow down just a bit. I could sense he was studying the water, although his hard body at my back confirmed it was still our weekend together that was on his mind. "I don't see anything."

"It comes and goes," I informed him. "You have to really watch. The light isn't much more than a dim flash you'd most likely miss if you aren't really focusing on it."

"It's probably a boat, or possibly a headlight from the highway on the east shore reflecting off the water," Kyle said as he lowered his head once again.

The light I'd seen didn't look like a boat, but the island was uninhabited and Kyle's lips on my neck had started a tingling deep down inside that was demanding my attention. "I guess you're right. Should we rejoin the others? Or perhaps you'd prefer to go back to your place?"

I expected Kyle to enthusiastically agree with the idea of heading to his place and was surprised when he didn't answer. I turned slightly and glanced at him. "Is everything okay?"

"It looks like we have company."

I glanced in the direction of Kyle's gaze and frowned. "What do you suppose she wants?"

"I have no idea, but I have a feeling this isn't a social call." Kyle released his arms from around my waist and took a step back.

I watched as Deputy Kate Baldwin, a petite and strongly opinionated new hire at the Serenity Sheriff's Department, approached from the nearby parking area. She stopped at the bonfire where the Serenity High School staff were gathered and spoke to Principal Greg Remington. They chatted for a few minutes, Greg pointed in my direction, and she headed toward where Kyle and I were standing.

"Kate," I greeted as she approached.

"Tj. Kyle."

"How can we help you this evening?" I asked in a syrupy

sweet tone of voice I was far from feeling. Kate was the polar opposite of my good friend, Deputy Roy Fisher. I got along great with him and had helped him with many local investigations, but Kate was a stringently by-the-book sort of woman who had no use for amateur sleuths. To say the two of us clashed was putting it mildly.

"Do you know Gina Roberts?" Kate asked, looking me directly in the eye.

"I do," I answered the woman I probably would have liked and admired had she not been an obstacle to my every move. "She's a math teacher at the high school where I work as a coach and physical education teacher."

"I understand this is a party for high school staff. Is she here?"

I shook my head. "I haven't seen her."

"Were you expecting her to be here?" Kate asked.

I frowned. "Actually, I was. We spoke earlier, and she said she'd see me here. But she never showed, and I haven't heard from her. Is there something going on?"

"Do you know what Gina's plans were between the time you spoke to her and the time she was to meet you here?"

"She told me she planned to volunteer at the regional wakeboard competition being held in Thunder Bay this morning and then she was going to grab lunch with a friend. I'm not certain what her plans were between lunch and meeting me here. Again, I have to ask, is Gina okay?"

Kate didn't even acknowledge my question before continuing with another of her own. "Do you remember Striker Bristow?"

"Of course I remember him. He was one of the prime

suspects in Judge Harper's murder investigation. What does he have to do with Gina? Why are you asking me all these questions?"

Kate glanced at Kyle and then back at me. I could sense she was hesitant to fill us in. I tried to respect the fact that she was a professional and we weren't, but there was no way I was letting this woman walk away without telling me what in the heck was going on.

Striker Bristow was a developer who came to town with plans to build a strip mall. When the mayor tried to push back he came up with a plan to blackmail him. It didn't work, but, personally, I had no use for the man.

"You may as well tell her why you're asking all these questions," Kyle said after a brief pause. "You know she isn't going to leave it alone if she thinks one of her friends is in some sort of trouble."

Kate looked at Kyle, and her face softened just a bit. Was the new deputy into Kyle? Sure, he was drop-dead gorgeous and smarter than pretty much anyone in town, but he was mine, and the new deputy had best keep her wandering eyes to herself. I was about to say something about women who poached in other women's territory when Kyle took my hand in his and gave it a gentle squeeze. It occurred to me that his smile and friendly demeanor had been calculated. There was no doubt he was going to get more out of Kate with his smile than I was going to get with a tantrum.

"Gina is wanted for questioning in the murder of Striker Bristow," Kate began.

"Bristow is dead?"

"Shot in the back. Now, do you have any idea where I can

find Ms. Roberts?"

"I don't know where she is, but there's no way Gina killed anyone. Why do you even suspect her of being involved?"

"The local highway patrol discovered an abandoned vehicle in a meadow near the intersection of Highway 89 and County Road 29 at approximately eight o'clock this evening," Kate began. "It appears the driver of the vehicle swerved for some reason, causing it to leave the highway and hit a tree. A male victim was found dead at the scene. While I won't have autopsy results until tomorrow, it appears he died of a gunshot wound delivered prior to the car hitting the tree. The victim has been identified as Striker Bristow. The car Mr. Bristow was found inside is registered to Gina Roberts."

"Wait. What?" A feeling of dread began to build inside me. "Gina has been in an accident. Is she okay?"

"We're uncertain at this point about her whereabouts or whether she's been injured. The driver-side door was open and there was blood on the seat, but we didn't find a second body."

"So what are you saying?" I asked as I tried to wrap my head around what she'd just said.

"It's our belief that whoever was driving the vehicle at the time of the accident left the scene."

"Voluntarily?" I asked.

"We're uncertain."

I felt a wave of dizziness as my heart began to pound. An image of Gina injured and scared flashed into my mind. I squeezed my eyes closed to shut out the fear and allow logic to return. If something happened to Gina I needed to keep a clear head. I needed to figure out what had become of her. "This whole thing doesn't make sense. Are you sure that the car where you found Bristow's body is the same car owned by Gina Roberts?"

"I just said as much," Kate answered with a tone of impatience in her voice.

"Why would Gina be with Bristow? As far as I know, she doesn't even know him. And even if for some twisted reason she was in the car with the guy, why would she flee the scene? It seems reasonable if she were conscious after the accident she would have called for help. And if Bristow died of a gunshot wound, who shot him? Surely you don't think Gina—"

"It's early in the investigation and we don't yet have all the facts. There's some evidence to suggest the driver of the vehicle may have been responsible for Bristow's gunshot wound, but there's also a very real possibility he was shot by a third party before either he or the driver entered the vehicle. Either way, the driver is a witness to what occurred. Now again," Kates tone hardened. "I'm going to ask if you have any idea where I can find Ms. Roberts."

"Maybe the driver of the vehicle was someone other than Gina," I continued. "Did you call her cell phone or check her house?"

"We did. Ms. Roberts isn't answering her cell and both her house and Mr. Bristow's apartment are unoccupied."

I put up a hand to steady myself as I tried to process everything Kate was telling us. The whole thing was so absurd I was having a hard time believing a word she'd said. Gina and Bristow? No way. I turned to Kyle who was not only my boyfriend but a town council member. "I thought Bristow left town. You told me the town council had decided to pass on his mall project after what happened with Judge Harper. You told me Bristow was a low life and everyone knew it, and he was destined to be nothing more than a vague reflection in the town's rearview mirror."

"I did tell you that, and I thought it to be true when I said it. I personally spoke to several council members who agreed that we didn't want to do business with a man who would try to blackmail the mayor." Kyle took a deep breath before running his hand through his thick blond hair. "But Bristow had been doing some politicking and the project was back on the agenda. From what I understand, he'd hired a new analyst and the proposal he'd put together appeared to be very beneficial for the town."

I threw my hands in the air. "I don't frigging believe this. How could that happen?"

"Bristow is smart and gregarious. He obviously worked hard to put together a proposal that seemed to some to be too good to pass up. I know I should have told you what was going on, but you've had so much on your plate with your dad's recovery and the extra hours you've been putting in at the resort since your dad's car accident. I knew you'd be upset after everything that happened, so I wanted to wait until I knew for sure how things would play out."

"I'm not a child. You don't have to protect me."

Kyle bowed his head. "I know. I'm sorry. I'll tell you everything, but for now I think we need to focus on Gina." Kyle turned his attention to Kate. "Did you check for her at the hospital?"

"We have," Kate responded. "So far Ms. Roberts hasn't been admitted to any medical facility within a sixty-mile radius." Kate turned her attention back to me. "Do you have any idea where she might have gone, should she have needed help but been unable or unwilling to go to a hospital?"

I glanced at the high school group gathered around the fire. The party still appeared to be in full swing, so I gathered no one realized the severity of the conversation Kyle and I were having with Kate. Eventually someone would become curious and wander over, but everyone knew Roy and I were friends—they might assume I had an equally good relationship with his new partner. I continued to remain quiet for another few minutes, trying to think as Gina would.

"I don't know where she'd go, but I do know there's no way she shot Bristow. Gina isn't a violent person. I don't know why he was found in her car, but I do know she's innocent of any wrongdoing. If she was in the car with Bristow she could be hurt. We have to find her."

"The Paradise County Sheriff's Department is looking for Ms. Roberts as we speak. I know you like to butt in where you aren't wanted or needed, and I strongly recommend you leave the investigation to the professionals."

"But—"

Kate cut me off. "There is no but. I know Roy tends to look the other way whenever you get it into your head to play amateur sleuth. I'll have no problem arresting you for hindering an investigation if I get even a hint you're nosing around in my case."

I suddenly realized Roy should be here and asked Kate where he was.

"He's in Reno this weekend for a conference, so I'm afraid you'll have to deal with me. Now, if you'll excuse me, I have an investigation to conduct. I'd suggest you return to the party."

"My friend is missing and may be injured or dead and you want me to return to the party?"

I noticed Kate seemed to flinch slightly before answering. "That's exactly what I'm saying."

Kyle closed the distance between us and put his arm around my shoulders. I didn't know whether he'd pulled me close as an offer of apology or to warn me to watch my tongue. Either way, Kyle had demonstrated on numerous occasions that he had my back, so I trusted him now. I stood in silence while Kate extracted a promise from Kyle to call if he heard anything. She walked back to the group gathered around the bonfire, and I watched as she spoke to Principal Remington again. She must have been asking the others about Gina because the people who previously had been drinking and having a good time squeezed in to hear what she had to say. After several minutes, Kate headed back to the parking area where she'd left her car.

I glanced at Kyle. "There's no way Gina shot Bristow. I can't explain why he was found in her car, but if she's involved in this, it's as a victim, not a killer. Gina could be in real trouble and I'm not going to sit around and do nothing. She could be hurt. She could be dying."

Kyle leaned forward slightly and kissed my forehead. "I agree Gina most likely didn't shoot Bristow, and I'm as concerned about her well-being as you are. We have very little to go on, which will make finding her tough, but I promise we'll figure this out."

"How? Where do we even start?" I could feel panic begin to build. Gina and I had only known each other for a couple of years, but in those two years I'd come to think of her as one of my very closest friends. Not only was she fun and easy to be around, but like me, she had shown a willingness to go the extra mile to help the students who had a problem they needed help working through.

"I'm not sure exactly," Kyle admitted. "But we need to try to remain calm and think logically. If Gina was with Bristow, as Kate suggests, maybe we can figure out where they were heading."

Kyle was right. Giving in to the panic I felt wasn't going to help Gina. I pulled my phone from my pocket. "Kate said she tried to call Gina, but I'm going to try myself." I dialed her number and waited. "It went straight to voicemail," I said.

"Her phone might just be turned off, but there's a chance it's been destroyed. Leave a message anyway in case she's able to access her messages at some point. Tell her you need her to call you, but keep it light. We don't know who might have the phone."

I nodded and began to speak. "Hey, Gina, it's Tj. I'm just calling to see where you are. I was expecting you to meet me at the bonfire. I guess you got held up, but we're all having a really good time and wish you were here. Anyway, give me a call when you get this message, even if it's late. You know how I worry." I hung up and looked at Kyle. "How was that?"

"That was fine. If Gina's okay and gets the message, she's likely to call you back because you admitted to being worried. If someone else listens to the message, you haven't given anything away."

"So what now?" I asked.

Kyle paused. I could tell by the expressions crossing his face that he was analyzing the situation and developing a game plan. When I first met Kyle he was so drop-dead gorgeous I was sure he was a model, or even an actor. When I found out he was a very accomplished software developer with mad hacker skills I couldn't have been happier. While I'm credited with solving a number of local murders, I couldn't have done any of it without Kyle's tech knowledge and ability to get whatever information required from any source connected to the internet.

"Do you still have a key to Gina's house from when you watered her plants while she was out of town last spring?" Kyle asked.

I nodded.

"Okay. It's after ten o'clock, so I doubt there are a lot of people out and about in her neighborhood. Let's grab the key and head over there to look around. Based on what Kate said, it didn't sound like anyone from the sheriff's department had searched her house yet. If we hurry there still might be something to find."

"Like what?" I asked.

Kyle shrugged. "I don't know. Maybe a note as to where she was heading this evening or some type of evidence that would explain why she was with Bristow in the first place. It's hard to know what we might find until we have a chance to look around."

"Okay. That makes sense. Gina's house key is in my desk drawer at the high school. I meant to give it back to her at the end of the school year, but I forgot."

"Can you get into the high school now?"

"I have both a key to the exterior doors and the alarm code." I paused and looked toward the others gathered around the fire. We were standing far enough away so we didn't run the risk of being overheard, but close enough to be considered part of the group. "Do you think we should tell them what we're doing?"

Kyle glanced toward the group, most of whom were drinking. "I think it's best to keep this between ourselves for the time being. I imagine that Kate asked them about Gina but I'm not sure how much she shared. We'll just say you aren't feeling well and have decided to head home."

"Okay. That sounds like a good idea. Should we call Roy to tell him what we're doing? I know Kate said he's in Reno, but I have the number to his personal cell and it isn't all that late."

Kyle tilted his head but didn't respond right away. I tried to read the answer in his bright blue eyes. "I'm not sure," he eventually said. "Roy has always been straight with us and I feel like we owe it to him to be straight with him about our intention to look into things regardless of Kate's wishes. But if he knows what we're doing, it's going to put him in an awkward position with his partner. He'll probably hear about the situation and may call you anyway, but I think I'd wait for him to make the first move."

I put my hand in Kyle's and curled my fingers around his. I was still irritated about him not telling me about Bristow's new proposal, but he'd been right that I had more than enough to deal with without adding to my plate a town council matter over which I had absolutely no control. I squeezed his hand both to find comfort in his strength and to let him know I wasn't really angry. What I was, I decided, was scared.

CHAPTER 2

Serenity High School was a large brown building with interior hallways that looked a lot like a spider. It was located just a block from Main Street and shared a parking lot with the county offices. During the school year the building was occupied for much of the day, but during the summer, when school was closed, there was rarely anyone around. I saw the lot was empty as we pulled in. My office was around the back, near the gym, so I directed Kyle to pull around to the rear. As I expected, the door was locked, so I used my key to enter the building. I was about to deactivate the alarm when I realized it had already been turned off.

Strange.

I shrugged and turned on the flashlight on my phone before starting down the dark hallway toward the physical education department. Maybe someone else had entered the building through another door, or maybe the last person to visit the building had forgotten to reactivate the code. Based on the stern reminders from Principal Remington to be mindful of the alarm, I imagined forgetting to reset it wasn't a rare occurrence.

My feet hitting the black-and-white tile created an echo as I hurried across the scuffed floors. The hallways were lined with lockers and free of windows. It was sort of freaky being alone in the building so late at night. I used my key to enter the gym, which led to the hallway where the physical education offices were located. I went into my office for the first time since the end of May, when school had ended, and took a quick look around. The piles of paperwork I had left behind were still waiting for me to complete when I returned, and the broken sporting equipment I'd meant to either repair or replace was still stacked in one corner. Classes started early in Paradise County and the new school year was only two weeks away. Perhaps I should take a few days to come in before that to get organized.

I ran my finger over the layer of dust on my desk before opening the top drawer. As I expected, the key to Gina's house, as well as the key to her office in the mathematics department were where I'd left them in the middle tray. I grabbed the keys and went back down the hallway and through the gym to the main part of the building. I was about to go to the door leading to the exterior of the building when it occurred to me that there could very well be a clue to Gina's whereabouts in her office. While I hadn't visited my office since school let out in the spring, Gina had seemed enthusiastic for the new school year to begin and I wouldn't be surprised if she hadn't already begun her preparations.

I entered the wing that housed the mathematics and science classrooms and offices and made my way to Gina's office. I opened the door, which hadn't been locked, and slipped inside. That seemed odd, but I supposed she might have forgotten to lock it the last time she was on campus. I clicked on the light and took a look around. There was something that looked like red mud on the floor that seemed to have been tracked in fairly recently, but other than that, the room was spotless and free of dust, indicating that Gina had indeed come by to start her pre-semester cleaning. There was a whiteboard in the corner with an equation on it I couldn't begin to understand. File cabinets lined one wall and the spider plant on top of the center file cabinet had been recently watered. Despite the somewhat surprising neatness of the office, nothing stood out as being helpful in tracking down Gina.

I opened the top drawer of her desk, which was as uncluttered as her office. There were a few pens and paper clips as well as a folder with the words *expense report* written on it. I opened the file and found sheets and sheets of numbers and data, along with a few bank statements. I had no idea if the information in the folder meant anything, the document on the top was dated the day before, so I decided to take the whole file with me. I tucked it into the crook of my arm and left the office. I was about to head back to Kyle when I heard something that sounded like footsteps.

"Hello?" I called.

My query was met with silence.

I took several steps down the dark hallway leading to the social sciences wing. "Is anyone there?" I called again.

Nothing. I continued down the hallway with only the light from my phone to guide me. I listened for more footsteps, but there were none. I paused at the intersection of two wings. I didn't see or hear anything, so I turned around and retraced my steps. Maybe I'd only thought I'd heard footsteps. It was sort of creepy being in the dark and deserted school so late at night. It wouldn't have been odd for my imagination to have jumped into overdrive. I took one last look around outside Gina's office, then continued through the deserted school to the back door. I reset the alarm, then headed to Kyle's truck.

"What did you find?" he asked when I climbed into the passenger seat with the file folder.

"Something from Gina's desk. There are financial and bank statements inside. I'm not sure if they're important, but there's a document dated just yesterday on top."

"I'll look at it when we get to my place. For now, let's head to Gina's. I'm hoping we can look around before Kate and her crew show up."

"Let's park on the street behind Gina's place," I suggested. "There are a lot of trees around, so Kate won't see your truck if she does drive by."

"That's a good idea. Can we get to the street that parallels the one Gina lives on from the highway?"

"Just take Fourth Street to Elm and make a left. I'll show you where to park."

Gina lived in a small, two-bedroom house in an older part of town. The lots were large, most of them dense with trees, affording each a modicum of privacy. As I suggested, we parked on the street that paralleled the one where Gina lived, separated from her property by a deeply wooded area. After a dark stroll through the thick brush we got to the back door. I knocked just in case Gina was home. When there was no answer, I turned the key in the lock and slowly opened the door.

"Gina, are you here?" I called as loudly as I dared. Again, there was no answer, so I stepped inside and motioned for Kyle to follow.

The back door brought us directly into the kitchen. "It looks like she's been gone since this morning," I said as I spotted coffee in the coffeepot and breakfast dishes in the sink.

We began opening and closing drawers and cupboards, looking for anything that might seem relevant as we made our way across the room toward the short hallway I knew led to the dining room and, eventually, to the living room at the front of the house. There were two bedrooms and a bath upstairs that could be reached from the stairs near the front door.

After a few minutes I paused my search. So far, I hadn't found anything that seemed even remotely notable, and based on the frown on his face, it seemed Kyle hadn't either. I stood in the middle of the kitchen and looked around. The cabinets, which were painted white, were clean and free of fingerprints except for the one nearest the coffeemaker. I crossed the room and opened the door. This cabinet contained coffee mugs as well as sugar, cream, and boxes filled with coffee pods. Gina loved coffee and seemed to drink it for a good part of each day, so I imagined the cabinet was opened and closed more often than the others. I doubted the kitchen would reveal any clues, but it did occur to me that there was a junk drawer in the house where I grew up that was a good place to look for interesting items. If I had to guess, the drawer near the phone hanging on the wall might be the one I was looking for.

"If you're on your way to the phone, check for messages," Kyle suggested.

"The phone doesn't work," I answered. "When Gina bought the house there was a phone already installed, but she told me she preferred using her cell, so she never had this hooked up."

"Hasn't Gina lived here for almost a year? It seems she would have taken it down by now," Kyle commented as he opened the refrigerator.

"I think she meant to but never got around to it." I opened the drawer I suspected contained the odds and ends everyone was likely to collect. This one contained a variety of pens and small notepads, coupons for nearby restaurants, an address book, a couple of matchbooks, a hair clip, and an assortment of rubber bands and paper clips. I slipped the address book into my bag, then opened the first of the three small notepads I'd found. One was half empty, though all the pages were blank. She probably used it to make lists or notes that she tore off and took with her. Another had names and phone numbers jotted down inside, and the third had rows of numbers and letters on the first page that on the surface didn't show any real pattern.

"What do you make of this?" I asked Kyle, showing him this notepad.

"I guess they could be abbreviations of some sort or possibly a code. It's hard to know."

I put all three notebooks in my bag just in case. Kyle headed to the attached laundry room while I continued to look around in the kitchen. On impulse, I picked up the receiver of the phone Gina had already told me was inoperable. As expected, I didn't hear a dial tone, but when I put the receiver to my ear I did hear three clicks in rapid succession. I pulled the handset from my ear and looked at it. Okay, that was weird.

"Kyle," I called.

"Yeah?" he asked when he returned to the kitchen.

"What does it mean if you pick up the receiver of an inoperable phone and hear three clicks?"

Kyle crossed the room and took the receiver from my hand. He held it up to his own ear. "I don't hear anything."

"Hang up and then pick up the receiver again."

Kyle did as I suggested. "Sorry," he said. "I still don't hear anything."

I sighed. "I guess it was just my imagination. I think I've seen everything in here. Did you find anything in the laundry room?"

"Not really. We can take a closer look at the notepads when we get back to my place. Let's see if we can find anything in the rest of the house."

We went onto the dining area and then the living room. Neither provided anything that could even loosely be labeled a clue. I followed Kyle to the stairs, my heart pounding with fear and anticipation as we climbed to the second story. I wasn't sure what we'd find there, but I couldn't quite quell the feeling it would be something unpleasant.

Kyle took my hand as he opened the door to Gina's bedroom. "It looks like someone has gone through things in here already," he said.

He was right. While the downstairs was fairly neat except for a few dishes, the bedroom looked as if someone had sorted through everything. The closet was open, and the dresser and nightstand drawers had been left open to one degree or another. I supposed the explanation could be as simple as Gina looking for a favorite pair of earrings she'd misplaced prior to going out, but my instinct suggested there was something more going on.

One box that appeared as if it originally had been kept on the closet shelf was on the floor, upended. I picked up a pile of old bank statements, phone bills, and receipts and slipped them back into the box. "I'm beginning to get a bad feeling about things."

"Yeah. Me too," Kyle agreed.

"When Kate first told us she suspected Gina had been involved in an accident that had left Striker Bristow dead, part of me didn't believe her. Gina's a teacher at a small rural high school. She's sweet and conscientious and I couldn't believe she could be involved in anything dealing with the pond scum who tried to blackmail Judge Harper. But now that I've had time to process everything, I'm terrified." I set the pile of paperwork I was holding on the bed and looked at Kyle. "We have to find her."

"We will. I'll finish looking around in here. Why don't you see what you can find in the other room?"

I wandered into the Jack-and-Jill bath while Kyle took a closer look at the interior of the closet. The counter displayed a toothbrush holder with two toothbrushes, a soap dispenser, and a tiny cat figurine that appeared to be for decorative purposes only. I opened the medicine cabinet. Inside were the usual items—mouthwash, deodorant, nasal spray, and hair gel—but there were also birth control pills and antifungal cream. The birth control pills were prescribed to Gina, but the antifungal cream had been prescribed to someone named Spencer Becker. I had to wonder who Spencer was. Gina had never once mentioned anyone named Spencer to me.

I put both prescription items in my bag and returned to the bedroom.

"I didn't find anything of note in the bedroom," Kyle said after several minutes. "Any luck in the bathroom?"

"Not really, although there are two toothbrushes in the holder and some prescription cream with the name Spencer Becker on it. As far as I know, Gina lives alone."

"So who's Spencer Becker?" Kyle asked.

"I have no idea."

"When was the last time you spoke to Gina?" Kyle asked. "I mean really *spoke* to her about her life and relationships."

"Not since school let out," I admitted. "First we were in South Carolina, and then my dad had his accident and I got busy covering for him at the resort. I spoke to her briefly this past week, but only to firm up plans for tonight. Nothing personal beyond the usual inquiries about one's health and well-being."

"So it's possible Gina is in a relationship she just hasn't mentioned to you."

I shrugged. "Sure, I guess." I looked around the room for any additional evidence that a man had spent a significant amount of time here. I didn't find anything of note, although I did notice something on the bedside table and walked to it. "Look at this." I held up a small sticky note. "It says 'Murphy's, eight o'clock.'"

"Is there a date as well?" Kyle asked.

"No, just a time and place. It's probably unrelated to the accident, but it was sitting on her nightstand. Murphy's is closed for the night, but I'll follow up tomorrow if all of our other ideas peter out."

"I don't suppose you know where Gina kept her computer?" Kyle asked. "We might be able to find clues to what she'd been up to since school has been closed."

My eyes grew big. "I do know. She told me when I spoke to her this morning that her computer was glitching and she planned to take it to the repair shop in town. I bet it's still there. I also bet Kate doesn't know it's there, so maybe we can get our hands on it before she does."

Kyle looked at his watch. "It's almost midnight. We'll need to contact the owner of the repair shop tomorrow. Maybe we should head back to my place and try to come up with a plan."

"We can't go there yet. We need to go to the crash site and have a look around."

"Kate and her crew have already been there," Kyle pointed out. "She said she didn't find anything."

"Maybe Kate didn't find anything, but that doesn't mean there's nothing there. The driver of the vehicle, whether it was Gina or someone else, is missing. What if after the accident Gina or whoever was driving her car was dazed and simply got out of the car and wandered away? She could be lying out in the woods somewhere, maybe bleeding to death."

"I'm sure Kate has thought of that and has searched the woods as well."

"Maybe. But I need to check it out for myself. Let's run by the resort, get Echo, and then go to the crash site to look around."

"It's pretty dark," Kyle said.

"The lack of light won't matter to Echo." Echo, my Bernese Mountain Dog, had been trained in search and rescue. I grabbed some clothes from Gina's hamper, which should provide the scent we needed.

"I guess Echo might be able to pick up a trail even Kate and her crew could have missed," Kyle acknowledged. "Did you look in the guest room?"

"No. I was going to go there next. Gina has a desk in the room; it doubles as an office."

I was about to head into the second bedroom when Kyle held up a finger, indicating that I should wait. He walked over to the window and pulled back the blind. "Someone just pulled up out front."

My first instinct was to let out a sigh of relief—perhaps Gina was home.

"It's a sheriff's vehicle," Kyle added. "It looks like Kate with someone else."

"Great." I glanced toward the bedroom door. There was no way we'd make it down the stairs and out the back door before Kate came in the front door. "The window," I said. Gina's bedroom was at the back of the house; if we could sneak out of the house without having to go down to the first floor, we might get away without being seen.

Kyle nodded and lifted the window. He removed the screen and set it on the part of the first-floor roof that hung out farther than the second story. I climbed out onto the roof and grabbed the screen, and Kyle followed, then quietly closed the window. We couldn't both replace the screen and close the window from the outside so we'd need to take the screen with us and return it later. I could hear someone enter the house through the front door, so I knew we had to hurry. I jumped from the roof to the ground below, stashed the screen behind the tool shed, and hurried into the woods with Kyle behind me.

"What do you think?" Kyle asked as we paused to make sure we hadn't been seen.

"No one came out of the house, so I think we're fine. We should be as quiet as possible as we make our way through the woods to the truck, though."

"I guess it's a good thing we parked beyond the wooded area. If we'd parked on the street in front of Gina's house, we'd be busted for sure."

"Things really were a lot easier before Kate came along," I whispered. "If Roy was here he'd be working with us, not against us."

"Do you think Kate would actually arrest us for trying to find Gina on our own?"

"Knowing her, probably," I answered.

"Then we'll need to be extra-careful."

I was about to agree when I heard a loud snap. "What was that?" I whispered.

"It sounds like someone stepped on a tree branch," Kyle replied, so quietly I was barely able to make out what he'd said.

I held my breath and listened. I heard another snap. This time the noise sounded closer. I hoped there wasn't someone searching the woods. If there was, we'd never be able to avoid detection.

The lights in the kitchen at the back of Gina's house went on. I scooted farther into the dense brush just in case someone looked out the window. I could see Kate and a deputy with dark brown hair walking around inside. I didn't recognize him, so I figured he must be a temp sent to help by the main office. Kate picked up the handset to the phone, listened, then replaced it. She motioned for the man to check upstairs before making a call from her cell.

"We need to get out of here," I whispered. "If Kate looks in our direction she might see us."

Kyle nodded.

I took a small step and almost jumped out of my skin when the rustling in the bushes indicated that whoever was in the woods with us was getting closer.

Kyle put a finger to his lips and I nodded. He crouched

down low and very carefully and slowly made his way through the thick brush. I followed, staying low too. After a few minutes Kyle stopped and slowly stood up. I did likewise. Kyle tapped my shoulder and then pointed to a clearing just beyond the shrubs we were hiding behind. I let out a sigh of relief when I realized our visitor was a bear, not a cop.

I came into contact with bears on a regular basis, living at the resort, which was surrounded by dense forest. I knew that they wouldn't bother you if you didn't bother them, so had learned not to fear the large mammals. But I also knew it was important not to startle the animal. We couldn't call out or turn on our own flashlights to announce our presence without running the risk of being seen or heard from the house, so I slowly took a step back, keeping my eye on the bear, which seemed to be ignoring us at this point. Kyle took a step back as well. The bear looked up and turned in our direction. He looked right at us before lowering his head and continuing with his meal. Once I was fairly certain he didn't consider us a threat, Kyle and I continued to put space between us and him, taking only a single step at a time and never once taking our eyes off the large predator. When we were what seemed to be a safe distance away, we picked up the pace a bit until we reached Kyle's truck. Neither of us spoke until we were inside the vehicle.

"What now?" Kyle asked after starting the vehicle and putting some distance between us and Gina's house. "Do you still want to go to the scene of the accident?"

"I do. I can't shake the feeling that Gina could be all alone, clinging to life with no one to help her. We need to hurry."

CHAPTER 3

Kyle merged onto the county road that led to the resort where I lived with my father and his fiancée, my two half-sisters who came to live with me after our mother died, my grandpa, and a dozen or so animals. The house was dark, so I assumed Grandpa was asleep. I quietly entered through the kitchen door and then headed to my bedroom where I thought Echo would be sleeping. He began wagging his tail as soon as he saw me. I motioned for him to quietly follow me. When I returned to the kitchen, I scribbled a note, letting Grandpa know I'd stopped by for Echo and would be keeping him with me for the weekend. I grabbed a couple of bottles of water from the refrigerator and then went back out to the truck.

Echo greeted Kyle and settled into the backseat, and we pulled away from the resort and onto the highway in the direction of the place where the accident occurred. The drive was a silent one except for Echo panting behind us. Every time I thought of Gina hurt, scared, and alone, my heart ached so badly I could barely stand it. I was deep in my own thoughts and not really paying attention to the trip, so I was startled when Kyle pulled the truck over to the side of the road.

"What is it?" I asked.

"There's a car behind us. I think it's been following us."

I turned and looked down the empty highway. "I don't see anything."

"The car pulled over and turned off its headlights right after I did."

"Why would someone be following us?"

I sensed Kyle's frown, although it was too dark to see his expression.

"I'm not sure," Kyle finally answered.

"Are you sure the car was following us, not just heading in the same direction we are?"

"I'm sure." Kyle pulled back onto the highway and executed a quick U-turn, heading back the way we'd come. When we came to a dark blue sedan parked on the side of the road, Kyle slowed down a bit but didn't stop.

"It looked like a Ford Focus, either dark blue or black. I didn't catch the license plate number," Kyle said.

"The plate on the front was missing," I informed Kyle. "I looked as we passed. It was too dark to see the plate on the back after we passed, but I noticed a dent in the front fender on the driver's side."

"Yeah, I saw that as well. It's pretty desolate out here at this time of night and I don't like the idea that the car was following us. Maybe we should head back to my place," Kyle suggested.

"But Gina..."

"I doubt we'll find her at the accident scene. Let's try her cell phone again. If she still doesn't answer, we'll go to my place and come up with a plan."

"No. I can't just leave her there. I know you think Kate would have found her if she'd been anywhere near the accident site, but I need to see for myself. Let's pull off the road and see if that car passes us as it heads back to town. If it does, we'll continue on to the scene of the accident."

Kyle didn't look thrilled with my decision, but he pulled his truck off the road, positioning it behind some trees. We turned off the lights and waited. Kyle took my hand in his. "I know it's hard not to worry, but that can cloud a person's judgement. As I've said, we need to stay clearheaded. We still don't know for certain Gina was even in the car with Bristow."

"I know that, but Gina didn't come to the bonfire and she isn't answering her cell. If she wasn't in the car, where is she? And if she isn't involved with Bristow, why would someone go through her room? I'm trying to keep a clear head, but I can't help picturing her hurt and scared with no one to help her. We have to find her."

Kyle squeezed my hand. "We will."

I sat forward and stared at the road in front of us as a car went by. "I think that was the car that was following us."

"It was," Kyle confirmed. "I was able to make out the first couple of letters of the license plate, but it passed too quickly for me to see the whole thing."

"What were the letters you saw?" I asked.

"CV."

"So we just need to find a dark-colored Ford Focus with a dent in the front left fender and a license plate beginning with CV," I summarized. "We've been successful when we've had less to go on."

"True."

"Now that the car has passed, let's go find Gina."

Kyle frowned. "Let's wait a few minutes to make sure they

don't double back around."

A few minutes felt like an eternity, but eventually, Kyle decided it was probably safe to go on. I kept my eye on the rearview mirror as we drove. The idea that someone might have been following us had left me feeling nervous and edgy.

"When did you first notice we had a tail?" I asked, nervously keeping an eye on the road behind us.

"When we pulled up at the stoplight on Main after we left Gina's house, a car pulled up behind us. At first I didn't think anything of it, but it's late and there isn't a lot of traffic, so I couldn't help but notice that the car that had pulled up behind us at the light made all the turns we did as we headed out to the resort. It went past after I turned onto the resort road and I didn't see it again until we came back through town and turned on to the highway. I wasn't certain it was the same car, even though it looked like it, so I pulled over to see what they would do. When they pulled over as well I was pretty sure we'd indeed been followed all the way from Gina's."

"Why would someone be following us?"

"I don't know, but I don't like it. I especially don't like that they followed us to the resort. I'm not sure what's going on, but I think we'd better watch our back."

If I wasn't freaked out before, I certainly was now.

Despite the fact that I hadn't slept in almost twenty hours, by the time we reached the accident site I felt totally awake, even somewhat wired. Gina's car had been towed away, but it was easy to see the mangled shrubbery and foliage in the path it had traveled between the road and the tree that had stopped its forward motion.

We parked and got out of the truck, and I held up the tank

top I'd taken from Gina's hamper to Echo. He took a couple of sniffs and headed into the woods.

"Gina," I called into the darkness on the off-chance she was hiding somewhere. "It's Tj. Are you here? Can you hear me?"

There was a rustling off to my left. Echo didn't respond to it, and it wasn't loud enough to have been caused by a bear or a person, so I guessed it must be a raccoon or some other small nocturnal animal. I watched the light from Kyle's flashlight on my left. I was about to admit defeat when Echo stopped and barked once. I went to where he was standing. There was blood on the ground and his paw rested on something shiny. I bent down and picked it up. "Kyle," I called.

He looked up, then headed in my direction.

"Did you find something?" he asked when he joined me.

I held up a bracelet. "This is Gina's."

Kyle took a step closer and shone his light on the silver chain with a delicate moon charm. He looked in to the woods, then back to the spot where the car had ended up. "So she must have been in the car."

I put my hand to my mouth. I wanted to scream but it would do no good. There was a part of me that until this moment still hoped that Gina hadn't been the driver of the car. Was she even still alive? I thought about the blood Kate had reportedly seen on the driver's side seat along with the blood on the ground near Gina's bracelet. I took a deep breath to calm my hysteria and glanced at Kyle. "Gina wore this bracelet all the time. I'm not sure where she got it, but I got the impression it was important to her." I glanced into the densely wooded area behind me. "She must have left the car either on her own or with wanted or unwanted help and then traveled in this direction."

"It would have made more sense to either stay with the car or walk to the road," Kyle pointed out. "Why would she go into the woods?"

"I don't know." Chills crawled up my spine as I considered all the possible options. "Bristow was shot; maybe whoever did it was on their tail. After the crash she might have been scared and tried to hide."

"So you think she might have been followed?"

"It's as good a theory as any. The person who shot Bristow might even have caused the accident."

"I guess that would explain how it happened."

"I think the trail goes off to the left." I looked at Echo. Once again I told him to find Gina.

Echo went on, and Kyle and I followed. I took Kyle's hand, walking slowly as Echo led us deeper and deeper into the forest. An owl called out from a nearby treetop as the creatures we were disturbing rustled in the shrubbery.

A coyote howled in the distance. Echo stopped walking.

"What is it?" I asked.

"It looks like there was a struggle here," Kyle said from beside me. "See the large area of undergrowth that's been flattened?"

"That could have been flattened by an animal. I've seem similar spots while out jogging in the morning. A bear or some other large animal could have stopped to take a nap."

"Perhaps. But there is blood on the grass, so I am going to stick with my theory of a struggle.

A tear trailed down my cheek. I quickly wiped it away. If I was going to find Gina I had to be strong.

Echo started down the trail that veered off to the left and

we followed. Eventually the path let out at the road. Poor Gina. The fact that the trail ended at the road indicated to me that Gina may have escaped the wreckage and then gone into the woods, where she was tracked and eventually captured. I leaned back my head and looked up at the dark sky. What in the world had she gotten herself into?

Kyle took my hand. "Let's head back. I doubt there's anything more to find in the dark. We can come back after it gets light if you want."

I stood perfectly still and looked into the distance. *Where are you, Gina?* Part of me knew she was no longer nearby, but another was terrified to leave in case she was just beyond the next grouping of shrubbery or lying unconscious in the nearby ravine.

"Echo?" I asked.

He sniffed the pavement where the trail had met the road and then laid down letting me know the scent he was following had come to an end. "Okay," I finally said. "I guess she isn't here." I took a deep breath. "I wonder what happened to her purse."

"Maybe the crew from the sheriff's department found it when they were here earlier."

I took one final look around, called Echo to my side, and then Kyle led me back to his truck. I looked at the clock on the dash as we pulled onto the highway. Two fifteen. "Let's go over to the impound lot."

Kyle looked surprised by my suggestion. "The lot will be locked up tight and there are watchdogs that run free when the lot is closed."

"A watchdog, singular," I corrected. "His name is Jasper

and we're buddies."

"How is it you are buddies with a junk yard dog?"

"Jasper's first owner had the idea to try to train him to do search and rescue. He knew that I had trained Echo for that very task so he asked me to work with Jasper. I tried to teach him what he needed to know but he had a short attention span and simply wasn't suited for S&R work. The disappointed owner decided to sell him to the owner of the impound lot and try again with another dog. By this point I'd bonded with Jasper so I talked to the impound lot owner and he agreed to let me take Jasper out for a day of fun every now and then. I'm afraid it has been almost a year since I've seen him but I'm sure he'll remember me."

"Even if you know the dog, doesn't it make more sense to wait and talk to the impound lot owner tomorrow? It sounds like you know him as well."

"If we don't look at the car tonight, we may never have the chance. Most of the time the vehicles involved in crimes or accidents are towed to the larger lot in Indulgence."

Kyle shrugged. "Okay. If you want to go to the impound lot that's what we'll do. Do you have a plan to open the gate?"

"Don't need to. I'll go over the fence."

Kyle glanced at me. "Are you sure about that?"

"Positive."

Kyle didn't look happy with the idea, but he headed back toward town. I knew Kyle often considered my ideas to be reckless, but even when he didn't agree with them, he always supported me. I hated to worry him, but sometimes it was necessary to take a risk to find the answers you needed.

Once we arrived at the lot we decided I would climb the

fence and check out the car while Kyle and Echo watched for any visitors who might happen by. Kyle had thought he should be the one to climb the fence while I stood guard, but I pointed out that Jasper knew me and didn't know him and would probably tear him a new one if he tried to access the lot.

"Jasper, are you here?" I called out after I'd climbed the fence but before I hopped off onto the ground on the other side.

I waited as fierce barking greeted my query. Jasper, a very large German shepherd, came running to the spot where I sat atop the fence, his teeth bared.

"Jasper, it's me. It's Tj."

Jasper stopped at the foot of the fence. He was no longer barking, but his teeth were still bared. He looked at Echo, who was standing beside Kyle, and then back at me. He must have realized I was a friend because he began wagging his tail. I slowly climbed down on the other side of the fence, talking to him as I did. "I've stopped by to say hi. Do you remember me?"

Jasper's tail began to wag even harder, his growls turning into happy whining.

I slowly placed one foot on the ground, then the other. "How are you, boy?" I asked, scratching Jasper behind the ears. "I guess you must think it's strange I came to visit by climbing the fence, but I need to look around. Do you want to come with me?"

Jasper barked once.

I tried to decide where Gina's car would have been left in the crowded lot. If they planned to transport it to the larger lot on the south shore at some point, they'd most likely leave it in the front, so I headed in that direction. When I saw the car I recognized as Gina's, my stomach did a flip. I don't know what I was expecting, but I wasn't prepared for so much damage. And so much blood. The driver's side door was too close to the car next to it to open, and the passenger's had been damaged to the point that it wouldn't open at all. But the window on that side had been smashed, so I was able to lean in and look around. I wasn't sure exactly what I was looking for, but I hoped if there was a clue to be found I'd recognize it when I saw it. There was glass everywhere, but other than a Cheetos bag I didn't see anything interesting.

At first.

CHAPTER 4

I shone my light into the interior. The light reflected off something shiny on the floor, just under the driver's seat. Whatever it was had slid down under the metal plate where the seat attached to the floor and I couldn't get a good look at it and didn't want to climb inside, so I looked around for something to use to net it. It was dark and there were a lot of cars packed into a tight space, which made it difficult to find anything. After a few minutes I managed to find a long rod with a hook on the end propped against a shed. I imagined the rod was used to do exactly what I wanted it for: to fish an object out of a tight space. I returned to Gina's car and leaned in through the window, being careful not to cut myself. It took several minutes of maneuvering and failed attempts but eventually I was able to use the rod to capture the object and wiggle it slowly closer. My heart began to pound when I recognized the object to be Gina's key ring. I knew it was hers because there was a tiny silver moon with a star dangling from it attached to the end of the chain, similar to her bracelet.

She *must* have been in the car after all.

It took a bit of effort, but I managed to work the key ring up the side of the car door until it was within reach. There were five keys on the ring: one most likely to her house, one to the car, one to her classroom at the high school, and a small one I suspected must open her locker at the gym. I wasn't sure what the fifth one opened, but my instinct told me it would be important to find out.

Once I'd done what I could, I gave Jasper a couple of dog treats I had in my pocket for Echo, then headed back to the place in the fence I'd entered the lot. I said good-bye to Jasper, then climbed back over.

"Any luck?" Kyle asked as he helped me down the final few feet.

"The car is a mess and I couldn't get inside without risking a bad cut, but I found Gina's keys. I don't know if they'll reveal anything, but I figured I may as well take them."

"I'm surprised the deputies didn't find them."

"I am too although it is likely the car was simply towed here and the crime scene guys from the county office haven't had the chance to go through it yet." I tossed the keys into the tray on the console of Kyle's truck before helping Echo into the backseat. "It'll be light in a few hours. Let's see if we can't borrow Gina's computer from the repair shop and then we'll head over to your place."

"Borrow?" Kyle asked.

"Okay, steal," I admitted.

Kyle hesitated. "Are you sure about this? So far we've been skirting the line between breaking the law and bending it, but breaking into the repair shop and taking a computer that doesn't belong to us is flat-out B and E. Maybe we should wait until morning and ask the repair shop owner for Gina's computer."

"Do you think he'll give it to us?" I asked, knowing the

answer all the while.

"No, I guess not." Kyle sighed. "But I still think breaking into the shop might be an unwarranted risk. Most likely the shop has a surveillance system of some sort."

I turned in my seat so I was facing Kyle. "I know it's a risk, but the computer might give us a clue to what Gina had gotten herself into. I can't get her out of my mind. I'm so scared for her. I can't just go home and get on with my life without knowing for sure what happened."

Kyle nodded. "I know. Me neither."

"So we break into the repair shop?"

Kyle didn't answer right away.

"Kyle? What are you thinking? Do we break in?"

"Maybe we won't have to. Do you know if Gina kept documents on her hard drive or an internet storage site like Dropbox or iCloud?"

"She saves everything to an online storage site called Cybersecurity. We both do. Sometimes we need to access work-related documents at home or vice versa. Why?"

"If everything is saved to the online account, we won't need her laptop to access the files as long as we know which storage site she used, her username, and her password. The same is true for her email. I don't suppose you know what she used for her username and password?"

"I don't, but we'd discussed how hard it is to remember all the passwords we need, so she kept a master list."

Kyle cringed. "Not a good idea."

I nodded. "Yeah, we talked about that as well, but after suffering through the frustration of not remembering a password when we needed it most, we both agreed it was worth the risk. I keep my list in my desk at home as well as in my desk at work."

"Please tell me the list is locked up and not labeled 'passwords.'"

"I'm not incompetent," I snapped back. I regretted it immediately when I saw Kyle flinch. "I'm sorry. I didn't mean to snap at you. I know you're just trying to help. I guess I'm letting the stress get to me."

"It's okay. I know you're worried. I am as well. Do you know where Gina keeps her list?"

"Not off hand, but I'd think it would be near her desk at home. We never did look around in the second bedroom she uses as an office. Maybe we should go back before it gets light."

"As much as I hate that idea, it seems preferable to breaking into the repair shop." Kyle made a sharp left and headed back toward Gina's.

"Let's drive by the house first to make sure Kate has gone. If the house is empty, we'll circle around and park on the street behind her property like before."

"That's a good idea."

The drive-by confirmed that the house was empty, so we parked on the far side of the forested land behind Gina's house. I put Echo on the leash and once again we snuck though the woods and got into Gina's home though the back door. I figured this was a good time to replace the screen, so I grabbed it from where I'd hidden it and went directly upstairs. I replaced the screen, then headed to the guest room, which had a small desk I knew Gina used from time to time. I tried to open the top drawer, but it was locked. I hated to break the lock in the event Gina was still alive and would return home, but I wasn't sure a hairpin was going to work.

"The keys I found," I said to Kyle. "There was an extra key. I think it might fit the desk drawer."

"I'll get them," Kyle said, and he headed for the stairs and the back door.

I took a few minutes to look around while I waited. Nothing really stood out as being odd or important other than the fact that there were men's clothing in the guest-room closet. I didn't think Gina had a boyfriend, so I couldn't help but wonder who they belonged to; although, there had been a second toothbrush and the cream in the bathroom, so maybe they belonged to Spencer Becker, whomever he was. Of course if Gina did have a boyfriend, why wouldn't he just keep his things in the closet in the master bedroom? I supposed there might not have been adequate space.

I opened the side drawers of the desk, which weren't locked. One was filled with pens, sticky notes, stamps, and other office supplies, another with files. The files were labeled and appeared to contain things such as tax returns, lesson plans, warranties, and other items found in many home offices.

I was about to take a closer look in the closet when I heard a door open and close, announcing Kyle's return. He'd made really good time, which meant he must have jogged to his truck. I waited while he made his way through the house and up the stairs. I turned to greet him and then froze in my tracks.

"Who are you and what in the hell are you doing here?" A tall man with blond hair and brown eyes asked from the hallway just outside the guest room.

Echo began to growl but hadn't moved. I momentarily considered siccing Echo on the man and running, but there was nowhere to go. "My name is Tj Jensen. I'm a friend of Gina's. We work together at the high school. Who are you?"

"I'm her brother, Spencer."

I frowned. "Spencer Becker?"

"Gina must have mentioned me."

"No, she didn't. I found your cream in the medicine cabinet."

His face mirrored his suspicion. "What on earth were you doing digging around in the medicine cabinet?"

I motioned for Echo to stand down. "If you're Gina's brother, why do you have different last names?"

"Gina and I are half siblings. Same mother, different fathers."

I guess that made sense. Gina had told me her mother had died when she was young, and her father had raised her. Spencer's father must have raised him as well. Still, it did seem odd that Gina hadn't mentioned that her brother was visiting when we'd talked. Our conversation had been brief, but I would think a visit from a long-lost brother would have been big news.

"If you're really Gina's brother, what was her mother's name?"

"Hazel."

Okay, that was right. I remembered Gina mentioning it when I introduced her to Serenity's postmistress, a woman also named Hazel. I was about to ask another question when Kyle came up the stairs and approached the room from behind Spencer, who turned around.

"Spencer, this is Kyle," I introduced them. "Spencer claims to be Gina's half-brother."

"I *am* Gina's half-brother," Spencer said, a tone of irritation in his voice. "Why are you here again?"

"If you are Gina's brother, do you know where she is?" Kyle asked before I could respond.

"She said something about a party for work. Given that it's almost four o'clock in the morning, I'm going to assume she decided to stay over with her boyfriend."

"So Gina does have a boyfriend?"

Spencer narrowed his brows. "If you really are her friend, shouldn't you know that?"

"We work together but haven't really had a chance to hang out for a few months."

"I see." The expression on Spencer's face indicated he didn't see at all.

"If Gina has a boyfriend, do you know his name?" I asked.

"She didn't say and I didn't ask. To be honest, even if I knew, I might not tell you. I'm still not sure you're who you say you are. I should probably call the cops and report a break-in, but I'm exhausted and would like to get some shut-eye, so if you don't mind showing yourselves out..."

I glanced at Kyle. I needed to get the keys from him to check the desk for the list before we left, but I couldn't think of a single reason to offer to Gina's already suspicious brother regarding why I needed to get into the desk in the room where he appeared to be staying. I was struggling to come up with a lie when his phone rang.

Spencer looked at the phone. "I need to get this. Please show yourselves out."

"I left my purse," I lied. "I'll just grab it and then we'll be on our way."

Spencer nodded, then headed toward the stairs. I grabbed

the keys from Kyle and used one of the keys on the ring to open the locked drawer. Sure enough, Gina's list was in a file labeled "recipes." I grabbed the list, folded it, and put it in my pocket, then headed into Gina's room for a purse because I hadn't brought mine. I found an empty one in the closet, then nodded to Kyle. I put the purse over my shoulder and we headed down the stairs.

Spencer was in the living room, pacing as he listened to whoever was on the other end of the call. I held up the purse and mouthed the words "thank you," then left through the front door. I supposed I should have been glad Spencer hadn't seemed to notice the lack of a vehicle parked in front of Gina's house. Once we were well away from the house we cut through a neighbor's yard and headed toward the forest where we'd parked.

"Do you think we should have told Gina's brother that she's missing before we left?" Kyle asked when we were safely out of sight of the house.

"I considered it, but we don't know he's her brother for sure. He might be, but he doesn't look anything like Gina. And if she had a brother visiting town, that would be huge news. I'm sure she would have mentioned it when we spoke, even though our conversation was brief."

Kyle raised a brow. "So you think he's lying?"

"I'm not sure, but my instinct at this point is to err on the side of caution."

"I agree. I don't know who he was speaking to, but he looked pretty agitated. If he's not Gina's brother, maybe he's working with whoever is behind this whole thing. It did seem odd that he let us go so easily if he actually is Gina's brother."

"Maybe *we* should call Kate and report a break-in at Gina's," I suggested. "If he's Gina's brother, he should be able to prove it. And if he isn't, she can get to the bottom of his real reason for being there."

"If we call Kate about a break-in at Gina's, she'll know we aren't staying out of her investigation," Kyle pointed out.

"That's true," I acknowledged.

"However, I have a burner cell at home," Kyle informed me. "We'll head back to my place and call 911. We can leave an anonymous tip about a prowler that someone will probably follow up on."

"Okay, that's a good idea. It's getting pretty late and we really do seem to be spinning our wheels. There's so much going on, I need to get things straight in my head."

When we arrived at Kyle's house, I fed Echo as well as Kyle's dog, Trooper, and then we went to Kyle's computer room. The first thing he did was call 911 to report a prowler at Gina's address. Then he ran a trace on Gina's phone, which was, as Kyle had predicted, still off-line.

Kyle glanced at his watch. "It's going to be light in an hour. Maybe we should get some sleep."

"There's no way I'm going to be able to sleep knowing Gina could be in real trouble," I countered.

"Okay. I'll get started on a search of the records Gina saved to Cybersecurity, but I'm going to need some coffee. Do you want some?"

I nodded, suddenly too tired to form words.

CHAPTER 5

Friday, August 11

I woke to the feel of the sun on my face. I slowly opened my eyes and looked around. I'd been sleeping fully dressed on Kyle's bed. Echo was lying on the floor next to me, but Kyle and Trooper were nowhere in sight. The last thing I remembered was talking to Kyle in his office. I looked at the bedside clock. Eight fifteen. I hadn't slept long, but I hadn't meant to sleep at all. I didn't see evidence that Kyle had joined me, but knowing him, he must have carried me in here, then continued to work.

Kyle must have taken off my shoes before pulling a quilt over me because they'd been placed neatly at the side of the bed. I sat down on the bench at the foot of the bed and gazed out the huge picture window that looked out on the icy-blue lake in the distance. Kyle had remodeled the entire house after inheriting it from his grandfather, and while he'd done a fantastic job in every room, the bedroom was my favorite. Not only did the large windows seem to bring the trees and lake inside, but the stone fireplace at the end of the bed gave the room a feeling of coziness. In the past month I had pictured my first night with

Kyle on more than one occasion. We'd light the room with scented candles and build a fire in the fireplace even though it was still the middle of summer. I figured we could open the windows if the room became too hot. In the past I hadn't given a lot of thought to the question of when to become intimate with the man I was dating, but Kyle was different. He was special. I knew in my heart that my first time with him would be my last first time with anyone, and I wanted it to be memorable. More than memorable, I wanted it to be perfect.

After I had slipped into my shoes I went downstairs. "I didn't mean to crash on you," I said as I walked into the kitchen, where he was working on a laptop.

"You didn't sleep long, but I figured you could use a short break. Coffee?"

"Please." Kyle handed me a large cup and I took a long sip. "Have you been working the whole time?"

"I got a few minutes of shut-eye, but yeah, basically."

"Did you find anything?"

Kyle topped off his own coffee and took his seat at the table. "I found quite a lot. Gina not only had a username and password for Cybersecurity on her cheat sheet, but she had them for her email account as well. I was able to access it and found several items of interest."

"Such as?" I tucked my legs up under my body and eased back into the comfortable chair.

Kyle took a sip of his coffee and then answered. "First of all, I was able to confirm that Gina does indeed have a half-brother named Spencer Becker. I found a series of emails between Gina and Spencer going back a couple of weeks. It seems he contacted Gina, introduced himself, and explained that he'd always wanted to get to know the sister he hadn't seen since she was a toddler. He wondered if he could visit. Gina replied that she was thrilled to finally meet the brother she'd only heard about in passing."

"I guess I feel better knowing the man we met was most likely Gina's brother and really did have permission to be in her house. Still, something seems odd to me." I ran a finger around the rim of my coffee cup as I considered the situation. While it appeared Spencer was exactly who he said he was, it seemed suspicious that he'd come into Gina's life after all these years just weeks before she turned up missing. "Do we know what sort of job Spencer has?"

"According to the emails, he's currently unemployed. If I had to guess, the reason he reached out to Gina when he did was because he needed a place to stay. I looked in to his background and didn't find any red flags, although I wasn't able to find a photo or current address for him. He doesn't have a police record and his employment history seemed pretty solid until a few months ago, when the company he was working for went under. I only took a quick peek and will continue to dig if you have a weird vibe about him."

"I suppose as long as there are no immediate red flags, we should focus our energy on finding Gina. You said you managed to get into her email account. Were there any that seemed suspect?"

"Most were work-related. I guess it makes sense that she would prefer to call or text friends. There was a file that I think might explain why Bristow and Gina were together."

"Please don't tell me they were lovers?" I groaned.

"No. At least I don't think so based on what I found. It looks like Gina has been working for Bristow."

Okay I wasn't expecting that. "Working for him? Why? In what capacity?"

"Again, I'm only speculating, but after the blackmail fiasco, he must have realized his project was in real trouble."

Striker Bristow had found some dirt on Judge Harper, who was acting mayor before his death, and tried to use a mistake he'd made as a young attorney to get him to change his stance and support his mall project. Judge Harper refused to give in to the pressure, but the fact that Bristow had even attempted to blackmail the acting mayor made him a bad guy in my eyes and, I thought, in everyone else's as well.

"So how did Gina get involved?" I asked.

"It appears Bristow contacted Gina about a month ago and asked her if she'd be willing to sign on with him as a financial consultant. I'm not sure how much of a background she has in finance, but she's more than competent when it comes to dealing with numbers, so I suppose that makes sense."

"She helped him with his new proposal?" I asked.

"It appears she did. I haven't had a chance to look at everything, but it appears she helped him cut costs significantly. Bristow used the extra savings to pad his proposal to benefit the town. He not only promised to build a park if his project is approved, but he had plans drawn up to build a new computer lab at the school."

"Sounds like a bribe."

"Maybe. But in this case the bribe was seen as more of an act of goodwill, where the developer makes an effort to give back to the community he's planning to move into. I know how you feel about the strip mall and Bristow, but I think he was going to get the votes he needed. The town really would benefit from another park and the school really does need new computers. And the gifts he promised are only the icing. If Bristow hadn't died and had received the go-ahead to build his mall, it would have done a lot to provide jobs and revitalize the community."

I couldn't help but frown. "Will you think less of me if I'm not as sorry as I should be that a man is dead and the strip mall will probably never happen?"

Kyle crossed the room and pulled me into his arms. He leaned forward and kissed me gently on the lips. "There's nothing you can do or say that will make me think less of you."

"I'm not sure I deserve that, but thank you." I took another sip of my coffee. "If Gina was working with Bristow, it makes sense they would spend some time together, but it doesn't explain how he ended up as a passenger in her car with a gunshot wound to the back."

"I've been thinking about that," Kyle said as poured me a second cup of coffee. "There are several scenarios that could fit the facts we have, but the one that seems to fit best is that Gina and Bristow were together, Bristow was shot, and Gina somehow managed to get him into her car and was going for help when something occurred to cause her to change direction. At this point my entire theory is speculation, but given that Gina's car ended up wrapped around a tree on the side of the road, I suggest whoever shot Bristow followed them, Gina tried to outrun them, she lost control of the car, and they ended up in the forest. She must have tried to flee, even went so far as to get out of the car and head for the cover of the trees, but the person or persons who were after them managed to track her down."

It felt like there was a lead weight on my heart. "If all of that is true, it means she's probably either dead or being held hostage by whoever shot Bristow." I looked into Kyle's eyes. "What are we going to do? How are we going to find her?"

"I'm not sure," Kyle admitted.

"Did you find anything else of interest in Gina's email account? Maybe something that would point to a motive for the whole thing?"

Kyle nodded. "I found a series of emails between Gina and a man named Carter Kline, but the most interesting thing was a file that's password protected. While I have no idea what's in it, it's the only thing I found with a second layer of security."

"Were you able to get in to it?"

"Not yet. The file is labeled SCABS. Does that mean anything to you?"

I shook my head. "Scabs? I don't think so."

"I'll keep working on it. It might help us to narrow things down a bit if we knew when and where Bristow was shot."

I placed my hands behind my head, lowering it slightly as I fought the fear and fatigue that threatened to cripple me. It had been hours since the accident. Was it even possible that Gina was still alive?

"Tj?" Kyle said, concern evident in his voice.

I lifted my head and looked at him. I tried to smile but I was sure it came out as more of a frown. "Maybe we can find out from Kate when and where Bristow was shot." I didn't think for a minute she would talk to me, but I couldn't help but remember the way she had looked at Kyle. "The more I think about it, however, the less sense this whole thing really makes. It seems to me that if Bristow was shot before entering the car, Gina would have called 911 instead of trying to get him to the hospital on her own."

"What if she didn't feel safe waiting?" Kyle asked. "What if she was at Bristow's home or office and witnessed the shooting? What if the person who delivered the shot was still in the area, or what if they left but Gina was afraid they were coming back? In that situation, she may have just helped him to her car and headed toward the hospital."

I groaned in frustration. "There are too many unknowns for us to ever figure this out."

"Unknown to us, but I bet the crime scene guys and the medical examiner have a better handle on the sequence of events."

Kyle had a point. "So how do we find out what they know?"

"Maybe it is time to call Roy," Kyle mused. "I wasn't sure we should at first, but things are really complicated. We need someone on the inside who can feed us information."

"Okay." I agreed that calling Roy was a much better option than trying to get information out of Kate. "I'll call him."

As it turned out, Kate had already called Roy, and by the time I spoken to him, he was on his way back to Paradise Lake. He planned to stop by to talk to Kate as soon as he got into town. In the meantime, he told me to wait to hear from him.

"He wasn't sure how long he'd be, but he said he was only ten minutes from town, so I guess it depends on how long his conversation with Kate takes. I hate to just wait around while Gina could be in real trouble, but I don't want to miss him."

"Do you want some breakfast?"

"I'm too upset to eat," I replied.

"Maybe, but you'll need fuel to get through the day."

"I guess you're right, but I'd like to clean up a bit before we do anything else. My hair probably looks like a rat is nesting in it and I never did brush my teeth last night."

"Your hair looks great as always and I have extra toothbrushes."

I picked up the large bag I'd been toting around. "I came prepared because I planned to come here with you after the bonfire."

Kyle looked more than just a little bit interested. "What else do you have in there?"

I smiled despite my worry and fatigue. "Help me find Gina and I might show you."

I'd put a lot of thought and effort into what was to have been my first night of intimacy with Kyle. I'd shopped for and bought new undergarments as well as a new negligée. I had scented candles and sensual oils, as well as a playlist of relaxing and romantic music on my iPod. It looked like all that preparation would be for naught, but there was no way my mind could focus on romance until I knew Gina was safe.

After I cleaned up I returned to the kitchen where Kyle was piling food onto plates. I hadn't thought I was hungry, but once I smelled the bacon he'd fried to perfection, I realized I was ravenous. Once the food was on the table, Kyle sat down across from me.

"This looks fantastic," I complimented.

"Thank you. I do scramble a mean egg."

I smiled and took several bites of the delicious food. "Earlier, when we were talking, you mentioned an email chain between Gina and someone named Carter Kline. I've thought about it and the name doesn't ring a bell."

"From the emails it appears Kline is a former academic

associate of Gina's. The emails indicated to me that she knew him well, so they must also have been friends, but there was a lot of discussion of equations and mathematical applications. The content of the emails was over my head, but if Gina doesn't turn up, it might be worth our while to contact him to see if he knows what Gina's plans were. There was an email dated this past Wednesday, so they've been in contact recently."

"Let's see if we can find out more about him before we try to get in touch. Right now I'm suspicious of everyone I don't know personally."

"I guess I can understand that."

Roy still hadn't shown up by the time we finished breakfast, so I took the dogs for a quick walk. Kyle had returned to the computer room and was completely engrossed in trying to hack into the password-protected file Gina had saved to Cybersecurity, and I didn't want him to have to stop what he was doing to see to the dogs. Besides, I was antsy and needed to blow off some steam.

Kyle really did live in the most beautiful spot on the lake. The huge mansion was built by his great-grandfather back when lumber was considered gold in this area. Not only did he have a spectacular home but it was perched on the edge of the lake in an isolated area known as Heavenly Bay. It had managed to avoid the logging operation, so the forest was lush with huge, old-growth trees. I loved walking along the isolated beach that lined the property Kyle had inherited. I could picture us someday raising a family here, although I might be getting just a bit ahead of myself, considering Kyle and I hadn't even slept together yet.

Once I reached the edge of the cove, I turned around and

started back for the house. I picked up the pace as I began to feel guilty for daydreaming about the life I'd have with Kyle while poor Gina could be dead or dying. I was almost to the house when a text came through from my dad, letting me know the physical therapy was going well and he and Rosalie should be home by Tuesday of the following week. I texted him back to say how happy I was with his progress. Being laid up and needing others to help with the most basic of tasks hadn't been easy for my big, strong father, who had hardly ever been sick a day in his life.

I wondered if Dad would be well enough to begin working part time at the resort again. My grandpa had founded the resort and was more than capable of running it, but I knew Dad was itching to get back into the driver's seat. Besides, Grandpa was getting on in years, and while he was fine if he needed to fill in here and there, the daily stress of being in charge would eventually catch up with him and could affect his health.

Back at the house, I gave the dogs fresh water and then joined Kyle in his office. "Any luck with the file?"

"Not yet. The security is really advanced. I have to admit, the harder the file is to hack in to, the more interested I am about what's inside."

"Do you think it's somehow related to what Gina was doing for Bristow?" I asked.

Kyle sat back in his chair and turned so he was facing me. "I don't know. The thing that strikes me as odd is that in general, Gina's security system is almost nonexistent. The presence of a single file that seems almost impossible to access is such an anomaly, it almost feels like someone other than Gina set up the security for it. Either that or Gina is a lot more talented than she wants anyone to believe, so she left a bunch of unimportant documents unprotected as a decoy."

"That would be a smart strategy if you were concerned that someone might want to access your account, but if that's what she did, why keep this file in the same online account as the other stuff? Wouldn't it make more sense to save it in another account altogether?"

"Good point. Maybe we should try to get hold of her computer and look around."

"Roy will be able to get it. I'll let him know where it is when he gets here."

Kyle returned his attention to the screen, typed in a few commands, and frowned. "What exactly do you know about Gina?"

"Not a lot. She's a really private person, but I know she moved to Serenity a couple of years ago when there was an opening in the mathematics department at the high school. Math isn't my strong suit, so most of the time I have no idea what she's working on, but I know administration feels lucky to have someone with her talent and knowledge base working at our little school."

"Do you know why she chose to work for Serenity High?"

I bit my lip and considered the question. "I'm not totally sure. Gina never really talks about her past. In fact, all I know about her is that her mother died when she was young and she was raised by her father. I thought she was an only child, but she's mentioned aunts, uncles, and cousins she visits from time to time. She's said she has a doctorate in applied mathematics, but I don't remember if she ever said what college she graduated from. And prior to moving to Serenity, she worked in the private sector for a while."

"I wonder what made her decide to teach."

"I don't know for sure. I know she made a lot of money in the private sector, but it seems something happened a few years ago that made her realize she needed a change. I'm not sure what was going on in her life when she applied for the job at Serenity High. She seems happy here, but I know she still does contract work from time to time. She took a month off last April to participate in some sort of top-secret project. She never did say exactly where she went or what she was working on, but I got the impression it was pretty important."

"If she's that bright and talented, why would she waste her time with Bristow?" Kyle asked. "It doesn't sound like she needed the money if she supplements her teacher's salary with private contracts."

I shrugged. "You got me. I guess Bristow might have been paying her a lot, but, as you said, it doesn't seem like she would be hard up for money and Bristow is such a snake. Still, I couldn't say what her finances might look like."

"She might have debt from her past or obligations we aren't aware of," Kyle offered.

"She might. But it seems to me that after everything that happened with Judge Harper, she would look elsewhere for work if she needed it."

"She may not have all the details about what occurred with Judge Harper. Few people do. There must be a piece of the puzzle we simply don't have yet."

"If you ask me, there are a lot of pieces to the puzzle we don't have." I paused when I heard a car in the drive. "It sounds like Roy's here. Hopefully, he'll be bringing some answers."

CHAPTER 6

Roy was born and raised in Paradise Lake, the same as me, and we had a relationship that extended beyond a law enforcement professional and the citizen he was sworn to protect. He and I were friends. We knew and trusted each other and, prior to his new partner coming to town, had worked together on several cases. Roy knew my strengths and faults and had a good track record in getting the best out of me. As I watched him get out of his car, I felt a sadness wash over me. I wondered if there would ever be a time when our relationship would again be as easy and unrestricted as it once had been.

Kyle invited Roy in and offered him coffee. The minute we were settled around the kitchen table, I asked him what he'd found out.

"After speaking to Kate, I had the feeling this was going to be a difficult case," Roy began. "She'd have a fit if she knew I was speaking to you, so it goes without saying that everything we discuss is to remain between us."

"Of course," Kyle and I both agreed.

"Do you have any idea who shot Bristow? Or where he was shot?" I asked.

"We don't have a lot of details yet, but based on the forensic evidence and the preliminary report from the coroner, it appears Bristow was shot before he entered the car," Roy answered.

"So he could have been in his home or his office?" I suggested.

"Perhaps. We haven't yet verified the location of the shooting, but Kate has searched both his office and his home, and she hasn't found any evidence that the murder occurred in either place. And she doesn't believe the shooting occurred at Gina's house either."

"It's all so strange. I can't begin to imagine where they might have been or how Bristow ended up dead, but you can't believe there's any way Gina did it."

"I don't believe that, and neither does Kate," Roy assured me. "Right now, we're operating under the assumption that the person driving the vehicle was trying to help Bristow and wasn't the one who shot him."

"Have you found any proof Gina was the driver?" I asked.

"We suspect she was, but we haven't found evidence that empirically supports that suspicion. We aren't certain why the vehicle ran off the road, but it appears Bristow died from the shotgun wound, not any injuries sustained in the accident."

"Was he even still alive when the accident occurred?" Kyle asked.

"We aren't sure, but the theory at this point is that he was already dead before the car hit the tree. We'll know more when we get the full autopsy back."

"What about Gina? Was she injured in the crash?" I wondered.

Roy leaned back in his chair and crossed his arms over his chest. "Based on the blood on the driver's seat I'd say it was likely. However, it does look as if the driver managed to leave the vehicle under their own power, so perhaps the injuries sustained by the driver were minor."

I let out a sigh of relief. Although I had no way to know if Gina was still alive and uninjured, at least I knew now she hadn't been gravely injured in the crash. "I found Gina's bracelet in the woods when Kyle and I took Echo out to look for her," I informed Roy. "There was a trail through the woods that ended at the road that feeds onto the highway on the other side of the forest. It looks like there was a struggle. Kyle and I think she was forced into a vehicle."

"It appears that's exactly what happened," Roy confirmed. "Although at this point we still can't know for certain."

"If we don't know who took her, how do we find her?" I asked.

"Kate has an all-points bulletin out on Gina and every available deputy is out looking for her. If she's still in the area, we'll find her."

"And if she isn't?"

"We're doing everything we can," Roy said. "Do you know anything at all that might help us narrow this down?"

I glanced at Kyle. I wanted to answer, but suddenly I was too scared to speak.

Kyle began, "It appears Gina was working for Bristow as some sort of a financial consultant. Bristow was a confident, arrogant businessman who got things done, but he wasn't popular. He had developments all over the world, and while I'm sure he had enemies right here at Paradise Lake, I'm equally certain he made enemies in other towns where he developed property. I'm not surprised he ended up dead. I think Gina may have simply become involved in something she wasn't prepared for."

"Have you come up with any leads at all?" Roy asked.

"If we tell you, will you feel obligated to tell Kate what we know?" I asked.

Roy hesitated.

"Look, I know you're in a tough spot," I added. "We want to find Gina and are happy to share what we know if it will help us find her faster. It's just that there are some things we want to get a look at first before Kate confiscates them and we're left out of the loop."

"Such as?" Roy asked.

I glanced at Kyle. He shrugged.

"For one thing, I know where Gina's computer is. I'll tell you if you can promise us that you'll let Kyle look at it before you show it to Kate."

Roy hesitated. "Yeah. Okay. Where's the computer?"

"She took it to the repair shop in town yesterday morning."

"The one next to the dress shop?"

I nodded.

"Okay. I'll go get it and bring it back here. But if you find anything Kate and I should know about, I'm counting on you to tell us."

"We'll tell you everything we find. You can decide what to share with Kate," I offered.

"That sounds fair."

"There's one other thing," Kyle added.

"I'm listening."

Kyle explained about accessing Gina's online account and the locked file he'd found. Roy asked Kyle to let him know if he found anything relevant to the investigation in Gina's files and Kyle agreed. Roy needed to get back to the station, and Kyle walked him to the door while I stared blankly into space.

"Are you okay?" he asked after returning to the kitchen.

"Not at all. The more we talk about this, the more frightened I become that Gina really is gone." I felt a tear slide down my cheek. "What are we going to do?"

Kyle sat down next to me and took my hand in his. "We're going to do everything we can think of to do."

"What if it's not enough?"

"At least we'll know we tried. I'm going to keep digging into the emails and files in Gina's Cybersecurity account, and try to create a timeline using them, along with texts, phone calls, anything I can get my hands on. Maybe if we can track her movements for the past few days, we'll come up with a clue as to who might have shot Bristow. If we can figure that out, we might be able to figure out where Gina is."

"What if whoever took her already killed her?"

Kyle paused and then answered slowly. "If whoever shot Bristow was going to kill Gina they most likely would have done it at the accident scene. Not finding her body then was good news. Chances are whoever took her is just holding her somewhere."

I took a deep breath. "Yeah. Okay. You're right. Sitting here being terrified isn't going to help us find Gina. She volunteered at the wakeboarding competition yesterday. That seems as good a place as any to start. Maybe we'll find her if we can map her movements leading up to Bristow's death."

"Do you want me to come with you?"

I glanced at the clock. It was almost ten thirty. "No. You

stay here and work on the files. You picked me up yesterday, so I don't have my car. Can I borrow your truck?"

"Absolutely."

"I'll see if I can figure out her movements leading up to her meeting with Bristow and you do the cyber thing. We'll meet up later and compare notes."

"Make sure your cell is on at all times," Kyle instructed. "And check in when you change location."

"I will. And I won't be long. Maybe a couple of hours."

I jogged up the stairs, splashed cold water on my face to wash away the tears I'd shed, combed my hair, and then called Grandpa to make sure he had things under control at the resort. He'd confirmed he didn't need me today, so I went out to Kyle's truck, then drove toward Thunder Bay. Whatever had gone down would most likely have occurred after Gina left the competition, but someone might have seen or overheard something that might lead to a viable clue as to the events leading up to the accident.

I paused as I neared the beach, where spectators were watching the competitors. They really were good. I'd entered the regional competition when I was nineteen, and while I hadn't won, I'd made the finals. I still remembered the thrill of landing the perfect jump or executing the perfect flip. While I still liked to wakeboard, I wasn't as daring as I once had been. Still, the energy created by the crowd was enough to provide me with the second wind I needed.

"Oh good, we have a new recruit." Polly Long, an English teacher at the high school, greeted me when I approached the judges' tent.

"I'm so sorry, I'm not going to be able to volunteer today.

I'm here to ask anyone who volunteered yesterday about Gina."

Polly frowned. "Is she still missing?"

"I'm afraid so. I know you were at the bonfire last night. I noticed Deputy Baldwin spoke to the group before she left. What did she tell you?"

"Not a lot. After she spoke to you and Kyle last night, she stopped by the larger group to ask us if we'd seen Gina. The deputy said she needed to speak to her regarding an investigation she was working on and wondered if any of us knew where she was. I told her I'd seen her here at the wakeboarding competition in the morning. She left at about one to have lunch with a friend and never came back. Do you know what's going on?"

I wasn't sure if I should tell Polly about the shooting and the accident and I didn't want to risk sharing information Kate wouldn't want me to, so I decided on a true but incomplete reply. "I'm not privy to all the details surrounding the investigation Deputy Baldwin is conducting, but I know she wants to speak to Gina and I've agreed to help track her down. The problem is, no one I've spoken to has seen Gina since before the bonfire yesterday."

"Do you think something happened to her?"

"I don't know, but Gina and I are friends and I'm worried about her. Did she say who she was meeting for lunch or where they planned to eat?"

"She didn't say who she was meeting, but she did mention wanting to try that new salad and deli place that just opened up on the wharf."

"Freshies?" I asked.

"Yeah, that's the place."

"Did she say anything more about her plans for the day or even what she was up to last week?"

Polly glanced at the water and marked her score sheet before she replied. I hated to divert her attention, but the contestants were currently engaged in test runs, which wouldn't count anyway.

"Gina didn't say where she was going after lunch, but I noticed she seemed fatigued. You know how energetic Gina usually is, but yesterday she looked rundown. I asked her if she thought she might be coming down with something and she said she wasn't sick, just worried. It seems an old friend was in town and his presence was creating all sorts of confused emotions she didn't have time to deal with."

"Did she give you any idea who this friend was?"

"No, but I'd say it was probably an ex-lover. People don't lose as much sleep as it appeared Gina had over a casual acquaintance."

Unless it was a long-lost brother, I thought to myself. "Are you sure Gina didn't mention a name?"

Polly shook her head. "No, sorry. You know, before you go, you might stop off at the snack bar and speak to Sheila. Gina worked the registration desk with her yesterday. They probably had more of a chance to chat."

"Thanks. I'll do that."

I headed to the rented food truck that served as the snack bar for the four-day event. Sheila Remington wasn't only the guidance counselor at the high school—she was Principal Greg Remington's wife. Luckily, the snack bar wasn't busy yet—it was early for lunch—so I was able to walk right up to the window Sheila was manning.

"Hey, Tj," she greeted me. "Any news about Gina?"

"Actually, that's what I wanted to talk to you about. Can you take a break?"

Sheila looked behind me toward the nonexistent line. "Yeah. Just give me a minute to tell the others I'll be away for a few minutes."

Sheila left the food truck and we wandered away from the crowd so we could speak without being overheard. There were picnic tables set up in the shade for lunchtime, so we grabbed one near the back where we were unlikely to be disturbed.

"What's going on?" Sheila asked. "I've been so worried about Gina."

"What exactly did Kate tell you last night?" I asked.

"Not a lot. After she spoke to you and Kyle, Detective Baldwin came over to the rest of us and said she needed to speak to Gina about an investigation she was working on. She wondered if anyone had seen her, and several of us had volunteered with her earlier in the day. But no one said they'd seen or talked to her after that."

"Did Gina say anything about her plans for the day once she finished her volunteer duties?"

Sheila paused. "She did say she was having lunch with a friend, but other than to comment in passing that she'd taken on some part-time work over the summer, she didn't say much." Sheila frowned. "Though she did mention she might have to meet with a man about a project she was working on, so she might be late to the bonfire."

"A project?"

"She didn't offer any details. I suppose she might be working on something different this summer, but she took a leave in April to do some sort of contract work. Greg might know more about it."

"Is he here?"

"No. He's watching the kids today while I help out here."

"Polly mentioned Gina looked run-down when she arrived to volunteer yesterday. Did you have the same impression?"

"Now that you mention it, it did seem like she wasn't her usual perky self."

"Polly said Gina had been losing sleep over the arrival of an old friend. Polly thought it was most likely an old boyfriend stirring up unwanted emotions."

Sheila hesitated. "It did seem like Gina had something heavy on her mind. She tried to hide it, but I could tell she was distracted. Still, she never said anything that would offer any insight into what was causing her to lose sleep."

I looked back toward the lake as I took a moment to think things over. So far, I hadn't heard anything I didn't already know. I needed more. "Has Gina confided anything to you she might not have shared with anyone else?" I asked. "You're a counselor, and I'm not asking you to betray confidences, but did Gina ever mention a brother to you? A half-brother to be specific?"

Sheila paused and then answered, "Gina did mention she had a brother during one of our conversations, but I got the impression she didn't know him. They had different fathers but the same mother, and Gina was raised by her dad. Why do you ask?"

"There's a man staying at Gina's house. He told me his name was Spencer Becker and he said he was Gina's half-brother. I'm not suggesting he's lying, but I had an odd feeling when I spoke to him."

"Odd how?" Sheila asked.

"I don't know. Something just didn't ring true to me. The whole thing felt off."

"I suppose having a brother unexpectedly come to town could account for the emotional turmoil Gina appeared to be struggling with. Especially one she'd never met until now."

"Yeah, I suppose. Kyle did a very preliminary background check on the guy and he seemed to think he was legit, although he hadn't been able to find a photo or a recent address for him, which is sort of odd."

"Maybe he should keep looking," Sheila said.

"Yeah, maybe he will, after he deals with a more urgent problem. There are reasons to believe the man staying at Gina's house is the real Spencer, who's her brother, though I can't quite quell this nagging feeling. This whole thing with Gina has me pretty upset. I imagine intense emotion could be messing with my normally reliable instinct about people."

Sheila placed her hand on my arm. "Maybe your instinct is off, maybe it isn't. If you have a bad feeling about him, my advice is to go ahead and explore it. If it turns out he's on the up-and-up, fine, but if he isn't..."

Sheila had a point. "I guess you're right. Thanks. I'm going over to Freshies. If you hear from Gina, let me know."

"I will, and you do the same."

Freshies was pretty close by, so I decided to walk there. The prettiest route was along the beach but the quickest route was through the parking lot. I headed down the path toward the parking lot when I noticed Kate walking toward me.

"Kate," I greeted. "Any news about Gina?"

"Nothing I am inclined to share. I hope your presence at the wakeboard competition isn't an indicator that you have ignored my dictate to stay out of things."

I plastered on a fake grin. "Of course not. I was only here to watch the heats this morning. I have full confidence that you and Roy are all over this."

Kate frowned. "How do you know Roy is back if you haven't been digging around?"

"I ran into him earlier. I'm late for an appointment. It's been nice talking with you but I gotta go."

I was sure Kate would pick up on my lame statement and realize that I *had* been snooping so I walked as fast as I could toward the pier, glancing behind me only once to make sure Kate hadn't followed. She hadn't, but she would very likely pick up the clue about Gina's lunch date, so I knew I needed to hurry to stay out ahead of her.

The restaurant was already open for lunch and there was a fairly large crowd when I arrived. I looked around for a familiar face. Waiting tables was a common summer job for high school students, and after a brief perusal, I spotted one of the girls on my soccer team speaking on the phone at the hostess station. I wandered over and waited for Sybil to finish her call.

"Are you here for lunch, Coach Jensen?" she asked.

"No, I'm not. Did you work yesterday?" I asked.

"Yes, ma'am."

"Did you see Ms. Roberts when she was here for lunch?"

Sybil nodded. "She was with Mr. Bristow."

"Did anyone join them?"

"No, they seemed to be talking business. Every time I stopped by to see how they were doing, they were discussing finances and strategies. It was way over my head."

If Gina had met Bristow here for lunch, it seemed obvious she wasn't trying to hide that she was working for him. That made me wonder why I hadn't heard about it before. Though I'd been very busy the past few weeks, spending most of my time at the resort, helping out while my dad was laid up. The truth of the matter was, there probably were a lot of things going on I hadn't heard about.

"Do you know what time they left?" I asked.

"I'm not sure. I guess around one thirty. Why do you ask?"

"I'm just trying to track down Ms. Roberts. We were supposed to meet, but she never showed up."

"Did you try calling her?"

"Her phone seems to be turned off. She didn't mention where she was going when she left here, did she?"

A large group walked in behind me, and Sybil picked up a stack of menus. "Not that I can recall. I only spoke to her for a moment when she was on her way out. She asked if I was ready for school next month and I said I wasn't. She asked if I planned to play soccer again and I said yes. She mentioned she'd been working on a new math program she wanted to introduce next year and I just groaned and told her math was definitely not my subject. When Mr. Bristow finished paying the check, they left."

"Okay, thanks for telling me what you remembered. If you see Ms. Roberts, will you tell her I'm trying to get hold of her?"

"Sure thing. You should come back when you have time to eat. The salads here are really good. The apple pecan blue cheese wedge is my favorite."

"It sounds delicious. I'll keep that in mind."

I left the restaurant and headed to Murphy's. I'd found the

note on Gina's bedside table that said Murphy's at eight, but it didn't specify a date. I figured it must be fairly recent, though, or Gina would have tossed the note by now.

Murphy's was a popular hangout. It had been my grandfather's favorite place to grab a cold one since before I was born, and some of my earliest memories were of sitting next to him at the bar, sipping a soda and watching a game on television. Although I'd visited many times as an adult, the smell of beer mingling with tobacco still created a welcoming feeling that in many ways was as soothing as a warm hug.

"Afternoon, Murphy," I said as I entered the dark bar.

"Tj. Must be a having a bad day. It's not like you to stop in so early."

"I'm not here for a drink. I'm here for information. Can you remember seeing Gina Roberts in here recently?"

"Sure."

"Do you remember when?"

Murphy rubbed his chin as he appeared to be considering my question. "I guess it must have been Wednesday."

"Was she with anyone?"

He set a glass of water in front of me. "She met someone, although I don't know his name and he didn't look familiar."

"Can you describe him?"

Murphy picked up a towel and began drying glasses. "I guess he was around forty. Dark hair peppered with gray at the temple. He had a professional look to him."

"Professional?" I asked. He didn't sound like either Bristow or Spencer.

"Wore a suit despite the fact he was sitting in a bar in the middle of the summer. It was a hot day too. I'm pretty sure he was the only one in here not wearing shorts."

"Do you have any idea what they were talking about?"

"No. It was busy, and I didn't pay any attention to their conversation. Is there a reason you're asking all these questions?"

I wasn't sure how many people I should share Gina's status with, but I'd known Murphy my whole life, and enough people knew Gina was missing that word was bound to get out soon if it hadn't already. "Gina seems to be missing. At least I don't know where she is, and she isn't answering her phone. I'm trying to retrace her steps over the past couple of days in the hopes of picking up a clue as to what she might have been up to."

Murphy set the glass he'd been drying on the rack and looked at me. "Funny you should mention Gina being missing. I ran into Hank Hammond at the restaurant supply in Reno early this morning and he mentioned he needed to get back because he had a meeting set up with Gina and Bristow at lunchtime."

"Lunchtime today?"

"That's what he said."

"Do you know what the meeting was about?"

"Hank's on the town council, so I imagine Bristow wanted to meet with him to get his support for his project."

"Okay, thanks." I stood up and took a quick sip of the water Murphy had given me. "I'll go talk to Hank. Maybe he knows something about whatever's going on."

Hank Hammond was Texas born and bred. He'd moved to Serenity about five years ago and opened a popular lakeside restaurant, the Beef and Brew. As Murphy had indicated, not only was Hank a successful business owner but he was a member of the town council. I knew Kyle had been trying to protect me by not filling me in on Bristow's plan, but Hank wasn't one to mince words. If he knew something, I was certain he would have no problem sharing the dirty details of Bristow's plan and Gina's part in it.

Unfortunately, it wasn't much after noon and the place was slammed. I was told by the hostess that Hank was busy cooking in the kitchen, and I poked my head in to tell him I needed to talk to him about Gina. He said he was supposed to meet with Gina and Bristow at eleven to talk about the mall project, but they never showed up. I asked if either of them had mentioned other council members they were going to speak to, and he said he knew they were making the rounds, but he wasn't sure where they were in the process. I told him I had some additional questions, but he was too busy to take a break but would call me later if things slowed down a bit. I thanked him and headed back to Kyle's.

CHAPTER 7

By the time I arrived back at Kyle's it was almost one o'clock. He'd used the notes he'd found in Gina's files to create a list of people who might either have a personal grudge against Bristow or were firmly against the mall project to the point where he felt they might resort to violence. I was glad he'd gotten the ball rolling. I'd hoped Roy would have called by now with the news that Gina had been found alive and well, but so far, Roy hadn't been in touch with news of any kind.

"Okay," I said after we'd settled once again around the kitchen table with cups of hot coffee. "What have you found?"

"I'd like to begin by saying I don't necessarily believe any of the individuals on my list shot Bristow, but all of them do seem to have motive."

"I get it. You aren't accusing anyone, just offering suggestions."

Kyle nodded. "Exactly. The first person who came to mind is a man named Byron Wildman. Wildman owns the property that backs up the piece of land Bristow wants to build on and has been vocal in his opposition to the project since day one. It seems that if the project is approved, not only would Wildman's fence back up to a parking lot instead of the green meadow with a seasonal creek that currently exists, but there's a dispute about the property line. Wildman says he's lived on the land for forty years and the property line was always the creek, but Bristow insists it's actually a good twenty yards beyond the point where Wildman's fence is now."

"Has anyone looked in to it?" I asked.

"Harper did before he died. He seemed to think Bristow might be correct, but after Harper died and it looked like the mall project was dead, the dispute sort of faded into the background. Now that Bristow was gaining support for his project again, the argument between the two men had escalated. I don't know for certain Wildman would shoot Bristow, but he's used a shotgun to run Bristow off the land he considers to be his on at least one occasion."

"So you think he might have snapped and shot the guy?"

"I'm just saying it's a possibility."

"From what you've said, I agree. Who else do you have?"

Kyle opened a folder he'd set on the table in front of him and opened it to the first sheet of paper. It looked like an invoice of some sort. "Clint Buford is a local architect who specializes in commercial projects. When Bristow first had the idea of building the mall, he hired Buford to draw up a design he could present to the council. After his design wasn't met with enthusiasm or support by the council, Bristow decided to go in another direction and hired an out-of-state firm to handle the project. Bristow never paid for the design he prepared, and Buford has filed a lawsuit against him."

"Sounds more like a motive for Bristow to shoot Buford to avoid an expensive lawsuit, not the other way around," I pointed out. "If Buford won the lawsuit, Bristow would have had to pay, but with him dead, Buford will likely never get his money."

"I don't disagree. Still, Buford is pretty upset. Not only has he been running around town badmouthing Bristow, but based on his behavior, it seems he might have been mad enough to pull the trigger. Before he died, I spoke to Judge Harper about it, and he said he'd looked at the agreement and the contract Bristow signed didn't state that the fee was contingent upon the town's acceptance of the plans. It really does look like Bristow was just trying to stiff the guy."

"Do you know the status of the lawsuit? At least up to the point at which Bristow was shot?"

"It's still on the books, but Bristow had made it clear to Buford that he should move on because there was no way he was paying for a design he couldn't sell to the town council. I don't have any idea how the lawsuit would have played out in court, but I understand Buford visited Bristow's office last week and the confrontation between them was so intense one of the neighboring businesses called Kate to break it up."

"You spoke to Kate?"

"Only briefly at the time of the incident, and only as a council member inquiring about a matter that could very well affect the town."

I wasn't thrilled Kyle seemed to get along with my archrival, but he was Kyle and tended to get along with everyone. I didn't comment but instead wrote down Buford's name on my list, below Wildman. "Okay, who else do you have?"

"Bristow was in the middle of a divorce," Kyle continued. "While his ex doesn't live in the area, she was seen in Serenity last week. It seems Bristow had stopped sending his support checks and she was here to collect. I'm not sure she's even still in town, but if she is, I think she should be considered a suspect until proven otherwise."

"I agree. What's her name?"

"Connie Bristow. Not only was she angry at her ex, but I would be interested to know whether she'll inherit Bristow's wealth now that he's gone."

"Can you find out?"

"I'll investigate the matter."

"Okay, I've added Mrs. Bristow to the list. Anyone else?"

Kyle picked up another file. It looked like he had neatly organized everything he had discovered, printing physical copies of documents neatly sorted by suspect. "Just one more. I'm not sure if there's anything here, but I already mentioned there's a seasonal stream that flows through the area where Bristow wanted to build his parking lot. A group headed by a man named Billy Sparks has been attempting to block the project for environmental reasons. I don't know Sparks well enough to know if he has violent tendencies, but there were several emails among those saved by Gina that were very strongly worded. I think it's at least worth following up on the status of the relationship between the two men."

"Okay. Sparks is on the list." I paused and looked down at it. "You've made a good case for all four people in terms of a motive to shoot Bristow in the back, but does it seem like any of them would go to the extreme of kidnapping Gina?"

"No," Kyle said. "And we don't know for certain that Gina's been kidnapped. We only know that no one has seen or heard from her in the past twenty hours, and it appears she was taken by force from the accident site. If we include her in the equation, things become a lot more complicated."

I looked at the list once again. "I suppose that someone like Connie Bristow might have felt threatened by Gina if she'd seen Gina and Bristow together and come away with the impression they were more than employee/employer."

"I suppose. It does seem like a long shot," Kyle admitted. "I wish I had a good answer to all this, but so far nothing really fits. As I said before, all we can really do is keep working on it and hope Gina's okay and we find her soon."

I ran my hands though my thick, unruly hair, trying to tame it. "I just feel so helpless."

"Yeah, me too."

"So what do we do now? Do we spend time talking to the four people on the list even though it seems very unlikely any of them have kidnapped Gina?"

Kyle furrowed his brow. He tapped a finger on the table but didn't answer right away. Eventually he spoke. "It does seem like we're grasping at straws, but I honestly don't know what else to do."

"Did you get into the locked file?" I asked.

Kyle glanced at the computer and frowned. "Not yet, which is odd in and of itself. The file has the type of security attached to it that you'd find with the military or government. Is there any reason you can think of that Gina would have a file from either of them?"

"Nothing I can think of offhand. She never told me anything about the project she worked on last spring. I think the contract was with someone in the private sector and I'm all but certain it had nothing to do with Bristow." I glanced at the clock. "It's almost one thirty. We have the entire afternoon to try to narrow this down. Maybe we should try to speak to at least a couple of the people on your list."

Kyle nodded. "Okay. I guess narrowing things down could be helpful. I have no idea if Mrs. Bristow is still in town or where she would be staying if she is, so let's put her on the back burner for now."

"Maggie's Hideaway is a member of the Paradise Lake Lodging Association. I'll send an email to the entire group enquiring if Connie Bristow is checked into their property."

Kyle grinned. "That's a fantastic idea. While we're waiting to hear, I have phone numbers for Wildman, Buford, and Sparks. I'll see who's available."

As it turned out, Byron Wildman wasn't available until three o'clock and Clint Buford didn't answer his phone, but Billy Sparks was in his office and available to speak to us. Not only was Billy an environmental advocate, but he was a local Realtor as well. His office was in one of the first multistory business developments to have been built in Serenity five years ago.

"Billy Sparks, this is Tj Jensen," Kyle introduced us when we arrived and were shown inside.

"I'm happy to meet you," I said as I shook his hand.

"Likewise. Please have a seat."

Kyle and I sat down on the opposite side of the long conference table where Billy seemed to have been working."

"I'm not sure if you've heard," Kyle began, "but Striker Bristow was shot and killed."

Billy actually smiled. "You don't say. When did that happen?"

"Yesterday," I supplied.

"We're speaking to everyone who might have had dealings with Bristow in the past week," Kyle said. "I understand you and he had a conflict over the mall he hoped to gain a permit for."

Billy nodded. "That's correct. The land Bristow proposed to use is environmentally sensitive, with a seasonal creek. In the spring the creek is part of the overall drainage and filtering system into the lake. Bristow's plan called for rerouting the stream to accommodate his parking lot. The environmental group I belong to is firmly against second-guessing Mother Nature. We believe the creek should be left in its natural state."

"When was the last time you spoke to Bristow?" Kyle asked.

"We spoke on the phone yesterday morning. He called me after he received legal notice of our group's intention to sue if he continued with his plans."

"I take it he wasn't happy about that."

"Not at all. In fact, he threatened to come over here and rearrange my face just before hanging up, but I never did see him. I guess he came to his senses and realized getting into a physical altercation with me would be political suicide. Our group is small, but we have powerful members, including two attorneys. I'm not sure we would have won in the end, but at the very least we would have tied up his project in court for years."

"When was the last time you saw him in person?" Kyle asked.

"I guess it's been about a week. He stopped by with some shallow threats to get me to back off, but he was full of hot air and I mostly ignored him. The lawsuit was already in the works, so nothing he said felt like an actual threat."

Kyle paused and glanced at me.

"Is there anyone else in your group Bristow might have been in contact with?" I asked.

"Not that I know of."

"Would you be willing to give us a list of your members?" I followed up.

Billy opened his desk drawer and took out a piece of paper. He handed it to me. "The membership for the environmental group is a matter of public record, so I have no problem sharing it with you, but I'm pretty sure I'm the only one to personally confront Bristow. As you can see, over two thirds of the members don't even live on the mountain."

I glanced at the list, which seemed to confirm what Billy had said. Other than him, I recognized only two of the ten names.

"Thank you for your time." Kyle stood up and held out his hand.

"Anytime. Can I assume now that Bristow is dead the project is dead as well?"

"I'm not in a position to respond to that," Kyle said. "Bristow owned a corporation that had shareholders, so there are factors beyond the involvement of one man to consider. I'm sure the town council will meet to discuss the situation."

"Well, keep me informed. I'll wait to dismiss the lawsuit until I hear the outcome of your meeting."

"Do you know Gina Roberts?" I asked before standing.

"Sure, I know her. She bowls in the same league I do."

"Have you seen her in the past twenty-four hours?"

"No, I haven't. Why do you ask?"

"It seems she was working for Bristow. We're trying to track her down to discuss her role in his business but haven't been able to locate her."

Billy frowned. "Gina and Bristow? Are you sure?"

"Pretty sure."

"Wow. I had no idea. Gina's such a sweet, caring person and Bristow was such a toad. I would never have guessed they'd be working together. I suppose Gina's influence explains the new approach Bristow took at the last council meeting."

I agreed but didn't say as much. Kyle shook Billy's hand and we left.

"What do you think?" I asked when we'd returned to Kyle's truck.

"I'm of a mind to believe him, and I'm pretty sure he isn't the one who shot Bristow."

"Why do you say that?" I asked.

"Bristow was seen having lunch with Gina yesterday at around one. The car was found with Bristow's body in it at around eight last evening. That means Bristow was shot between one and eight. We can get the exact time from Roy, but I think it was probably closer to eight. I noticed Billy's desk calendar. Written on yesterday's date was *Realtor training in Reno*. I can check to verify that he was there, but according to his calendar, the training ran from noon to six p.m. I doubt he would have made it back to town in time to shoot Bristow before his body was found in Gina's car."

"He might have left the training early," I pointed out. "Or he could have skipped it altogether."

"He might have, but it will be easy to check. I do have an idea which should have occurred to me before."

"Oh, and what is that?" I asked as I buckled my seatbelt.

"When I mentioned that Bristow had a corporation I realized that he also has a corporate office. Maybe we should take a look around. We might get a better idea as to what he was up to on the day he died."

"That's actually a really good idea. Do you think we can get in?"

"I don't know, but it wouldn't hurt to try."

"Okay, I'll drive while you call the Realtors Association to verify Billy Sparks's attendance at the training session."

Once Kyle confirmed he was not only there for the training but stayed for the dinner afterward, I mentally crossed him off our list.

Bristow's office was located in a commercial building in the old part of town. I parked in the lot and then Kyle and I headed toward the three-story complex that housed six businesses. Bristow had a small office on the ground floor. It was locked, as we should have expected it would be.

"Can I help you?" A woman asked after coming into the hallway from the office next to Bristow's.

"I don't suppose you have a key to the office next door?" Kyle asked.

"I don't but Frank will."

"Frank?"

"He works in the insurance office on the third floor. He's sort of the building manager."

"Okay, thank you." Kyle graced the woman with a smile and we headed up the stairs.

Luckily Frank knew Kyle from the town council and was happy to provide him with a key to the office after he explained that he was there on official town business.

"I can't believe that guy just gave you the key," I said as we headed back down the stairs.

"Did you see the woman in his office?"

Kyle and I had entered through the reception area. The

door to Frank's office was open but he had come into the reception area to talk to us. I tried to remember who had been sitting at the desk across from Frank. "No, I didn't notice. I assumed she was a client."

"She may have been a client, but she was also drop-dead gorgeous, and she had on the lowest cut tank top I've seen anywhere outside of the beach."

"So you think she might have had things on her mind other than insurance."

"That would be my guess," Kyle said as he used the key to open the door to Bristow's office. "Not only did he hand over the key without really asking any questions, but he informed me he had a client and would be in conference and I should just leave the key on the reception desk when I was finished."

"So he was going to have sex right there in his office?"

Kyle winked at me but didn't really answer. "Why don't you look through the things in and on his desk. I'll see if I can access his computer."

Kyle logged on but the computer was password protected. Given enough time he could get in, but time was one thing we did not have. I opened and closed the desk drawers, which weren't locked, but all I was able to find were random items such as pens, paperclips, sticky notes, and other unimportant items. I did notice that he had a note on his desk calendar to have lunch with Gina on Thursday, which we already knew, but there was also a note to meet Doug at five. Doug who?

"Do you know anyone named Doug?" I asked Kyle.

"I know several people named Doug. Why?"

"There's a note on the desk to meet Doug at five on the day he died."

"Bristow has an employee named Doug. He's some sort of an assistant. I've spoken to him on several occasions. He works out of his corporate office and only comes to Serenity on occasion. I suppose he might have been in town."

"Yeah, probably. Did you find anything?"

"Everything is locked. I could probably break in, but at this point I don't think that's the best move." Kyle glanced at his watch. "It's after three. Let's head over to see what Byron Wildman has to say for himself."

CHAPTER 8

Byron Wildman lived on a large piece of property that had been left in its natural state for generations. Not only was it densely forested, but there was a natural spring that encouraged wildlife to hang out in the area. Wildman was outside working on an old Ford truck when we arrived.

"Can I help ya?" Wildman asked after we left Kyle's truck. He looked to be in his late sixties and wore an old gray T-shirt under stained overalls.

"My name is Kyle Donovan. I'm a town council member. I called earlier about speaking to you about Striker Bristow."

"Yeah, I remember." Wildman began wiping his hands on a greasy rag. "What do you want to know?"

"I understand you've been involved in a dispute with Bristow regarding the property line separating your lot and the one he's proposed to develop."

"Dispute my ass. A dispute implies there are two sides. The fact of the matter is, that big-city snake in the grass is trying to steal my property. The creek is and always has been the property line. Everyone knows that."

"I can understand your frustration," Kyle said in a tone that I felt conveyed real sympathy. "I've been out of town and am trying to get up-to-date with the issues regarding the proposed development. I understand you've encountered Bristow trespassing on your property."

"Damn right I have. The man has no sense of propriety. When I asked him to leave, he laughed in my face and told me to get on home where I belonged. He didn't seem to understand that I *was* home. He was the one who needed to get. Talk about a stubborn fool. Nothing I said could get him to vacate my property until I introduced him to Old Remi."

"Old Remi?" I asked.

"The rifle my pappy left me. Doesn't work anymore. Hasn't for quite some time. But Bristow didn't know that. I pulled out Old Remi and pointed it at his head and he went running. Haven't seen him since."

"It's nice your dad handed his gun down to you," Kyle said. "Based on the name I'm assuming it's a Remington?"

"Yup. A Rolling Block."

"Very nice," Kyle responded. "My grandpa had a Remington. I'm not sure what ever happened to it. It didn't work either, but he was a collector and had other guns that did work."

"I'm not really a collector. I just have the one for sentimental value."

"You don't have a rifle for hunting or personal security?" I asked.

"I don't hunt, and until recently I haven't felt the need for personal security." Wildman looked at Kyle. "So about this Bristow fellow...I sure hope the council isn't going to get swept up in his sweet-talking ways. He can't be trusted. He's a liar and a cheat and in my opinion, he should be run out of town."

"I'll keep that in mind," Kyle answered.

It seemed obvious Wildman had no idea Bristow was dead. Unless he was a heck of an actor, which I doubted, he most likely wasn't the one who shot him. Kyle chatted with him for a few more minutes and then we made our excuses and left.

"So, what now?" Kyle asked as he pulled back onto the highway.

"Let me check my emails to see if anyone has gotten back to me about Mrs. Bristow." I pulled my phone out of my pocket, then pulled up my emails. "Bingo. It looks like she's staying at the Serenity Motor Inn."

"Should we head there now?" Kyle asked.

I turned slightly toward Kyle. "No time like the present. I also have a missed call from Jenna. I'd better call her back."

I hit Redial and waited for her to pick up. Jenna, her mother Helen, her daughters Kristi and Kari, and my sisters had left town yesterday morning with two dogs and a whole lot of camping equipment. I'd worried they might have bitten off more than they could chew, and I'd meant to check in anyway.

"Hey Jen, it's Tj. Sorry I missed your call. How's camping?"

I could hear the sound of dogs barking in the background as Jenna answered. "Yesterday was pretty intense, but now that we have all the equipment set up, we're actually having a good time. Mom took the girls and dogs down to the lake so I could have a few minutes to regroup."

"I hear dogs in the background. Are those ours?"

"No. There's a group camping at the next site over. Three men and eight preteen boys. They brought at least five dogs with them, but so far ours and theirs are getting along fine, and I get the feeling Kristi and Ashley feel like they've arrived at a cute-boy smorgasbord."

"That's just great," I groaned. "I don't think I'm quite ready for Ashley to be into the boy-crazy phase. I feel like she's still my little girl."

"She is your little girl, but she's also a young woman," Jenna reminded me.

"I guess. It's too bad Dennis had to work and Bookman didn't want to go," I said, referring to Jenna's husband and Helen's fiancé. "It'd be nice to have some men around to ward off the boys."

"Mom and I can ward off anyone who comes sniffing around," Jenna defended. "Still, it definitely would have been easier to get everything set up with a couple of extra pairs of hands. I think we'll be fine now, though. I'm calling because I just spoke to Dennis and he told me about Gina. Has she been found?"

"Not yet. Kyle and I are working on it, separately from Roy and Kate. I'm really worried. It feels like she's simply disappeared."

"Should we come back? Is there anything I could do to help?"

"Honestly, keeping the girls occupied is the most helpful thing you can do. You haven't spoken to Gina recently have you?"

Jenna didn't answer.

"Jen? Are you still there? Did I lose you?"

"I'm here. And I have seen Gina. She was at the restaurant on Wednesday." Jenna meant the Antiquery, the restaurant she owned.

"Was she there with someone? Did you speak to her?"

Jenna paused again before answering. "I was in the kitchen and didn't speak to her or even communicate with her, other than to wave from behind the pickup window."

"Was she alone?"

"No," Jenna answered. "She wasn't."

I frowned. "Okay, what's going on? Why are you acting so weird about this? Was she with Bristow? I bet you're thinking I'll be upset to hear she was with him, but I already know she was working for him."

"Gina was working for Bristow?" Jenna sounded genuinely surprised. "Why?"

"I'm not sure yet."

"I guess that explains why they were together at the time of the accident. When Dennis told me Bristow was dead and Gina was missing and it appeared they'd been in the same car, I was more than just a little confused."

"How does Dennis know all that anyway?" I asked.

"He's the captain of the Serenity Fire Department. He has connections."

I leaned back in my seat. "I guess that makes sense. So if Gina wasn't with Bristow when you saw them in the Antiquery on Wednesday, who was she with?"

"I'm not sure I should tell you this, but she was with Hunter."

I narrowed my gaze. "My Hunter?"

"Yeah. I didn't hear what they were talking about, but it looked as if they were having a pretty intense conversation. I even saw Hunter take her hand in his and give it a squeeze."

I don't know why I should be so surprised, but I was. Hunter was my ex. I'd broken up with him for the second time this past spring. Hunter and I were still friends and I had Kyle now, so I wasn't sure why the thought of Hunter and Gina together bothered me, but it did. I glanced at Kyle. He was looking at me with a frown on his face.

I plastered on a fake smile and returned to my conversation with Jenna. "That's great. Really. I'm happy for them. I heard Gina had a boyfriend, which surprised me. I guess now I know why she didn't mention it when we spoke on the phone. She probably wanted to tell me in person."

"I guess," Jenna said, a tone of doubt in her voice.

"I wonder if he knows what's going on."

"I'm sure he does," Jenna said. "Bristow's body must have been taken to the hospital for the autopsy."

Hunter was the head of the hospital.

"That doesn't mean he knows about Gina. I should call him."

"I guess that might be a good idea. Call me later if you want to talk. You know I'm always here for you."

"I know, and that means a lot to me." I signed off and hung up.

I turned and looked at Kyle, who was still driving, so only had part of his focus on me.

"So, what's going on?" he asked.

"Jenna said Gina and Hunter had lunch at the Antiquery on Wednesday. I should call him. I'm not sure he knows what's going on."

"Yeah, why don't you? We'll be at the inn in just a few minutes. I'll find a spot to park while you make your call."

I took a deep breath and dialed Hunter's number. I hadn't seen or even spoken to him since my dad had been released from the hospital. I loved Hunter and he was one of my best friends, but our on-again, off-again relationship had put a bit of a strain on our friendship. Still, we had a history, and I didn't want things to be weird between us.

"Tj?" Hunter asked when he answered his cell. "Is your dad okay?"

"He's great. I'm calling to ask about Gina."

"Gina? What about Gina?"

"I guess you heard Striker Bristow is dead."

"I heard."

"But I don't know if you're aware his body was found in Gina's car."

My statement was met with silence.

"Hunter?" I asked.

"Are you sure?" he asked.

"I'm sure. He was the passenger and the driver hasn't been found. We are operating under the assumption that was Gina, and whoever shot Bristow kidnapped her. Kyle and I have been working on finding out what happened to her, but so far we've hit one dead end after another."

"Oh God. Poor Gina. Can I help?"

"Maybe," I answered. "I spoke to Jenna, and she said you had lunch with Gina at the Antiquery on Wednesday."

"We did. Gina called and asked me to meet her. She had a problem and thought I might be able to help her."

"What kind of a problem?" I asked.

Hunter hesitated.

"Please. It could be important."

"Evidently, she has a half-brother she hadn't seen since she was a toddler. He contacted her a week or two ago and asked if he could come to Paradise Lake to see her. She agreed, but when he got here she wasn't sure she made the right decision."

"Why?"

Kyle had parked the truck in front of the inn and turned the engine off. Now he was sitting back, waiting.

"She suspected the man staying at her house might not be her brother," Hunter informed me. "He showed up with a prescription cream in her brother's name, but when she asked for ID, he told her he'd lost his wallet and didn't have any. She wanted to give him the benefit of the doubt, so she let him stay with her, but there were some things he said that didn't line up. She didn't want to confront him in case he really was her brother. She was afraid if he really was Spencer, she'd create bad blood between them. But she wanted to know the truth."

"So she went to you?" I asked.

"She wanted to know if I'd be able to do some genetic testing. I told her there were firms that did that sort to thing, but she wanted an answer right away. She hoped I could give her an immediate answer if she brought in both her and her brother's hairbrushes or toothbrushes."

"Can you get an answer right away?" I asked.

"No. We don't have the kind of equipment that would be required to do genetic testing in any amount of time. We send all our samples out."

I took a moment to process that. "So how did you leave things?" I asked.

"Gina was really upset. She said she was concerned that the man in her house was after something, although she didn't specify what that might be. She didn't want to send away samples and then have it take weeks for a reply, so I took the hair she'd brought with her and sent it to the lab we use with a rush on it."

"Did you hear back?"

"Not yet. Even a rush takes time. Do you have reason to believe she was right?" Hunter asked. "Do you think the man living in her house is responsible for the fact that she's missing?"

"I don't know. I met him, and my first impression was that something wasn't right. My gut tells me the man contacted Gina for a reason other than the desire to meet his long-lost sister. Will you call me when the results of the genetic test come back?"

"Yeah, I can do that. And if you find Gina or get an update on the situation, will you call me?"

"Of course," I promised. "I gotta go, but let's talk later."

"Okay...but Tj, if you need anything, anything at all, call me."

It did my heart good to know I could still depend on Hunter. "I will. Kyle and I are doing some interviews this afternoon. Hopefully we'll know more by the end of the day."

I hung up and turned to Kyle. "Gina asked Hunter to do a genetic test comparing her DNA with Spencer's. She suspected he might not be her brother."

"If you think something's off and Gina thought something was off, I'd say something's off."

"I'm going to call Roy to tell him what I just found out from Hunter," I said. "Then we'll go in to see if Connie Bristow is around. A conversation with Bristow's ex could be revealing."

CHAPTER 9

The Serenity Motor Inn was about a mile out of town, perched quite spectacularly on the banks of the Paradise River. In the spring, white-water rafters gathered here, because the inn was an ideal launching point for daylong float trips through the dense forest, and in the summer, it appealed to vacationers who wanted to be near the water but away from the crowds who swarmed the beaches around the lake. The inn was owned by Colin Welsh, who'd bought it over a dozen years back and was an active member of the Paradise Lake Lodging Association. His children had attended Serenity High School, so I knew him fairly well.

"Thank you for answering my email," I said to him when we entered the lobby. I gestured to Kyle. "You know Kyle."

Colin stuck out his hand and Kyle offered his in return. "How can I help you?"

"I'm not sure if you've heard, but Striker Bristow has been murdered," I began.

He nodded. "The new deputy was by this morning to speak to Mrs. Bristow."

"Kyle and I have a few questions of our own and were hoping she'd be willing to speak to us as well," I replied.

"I sort of figured that was what you were up to. I don't know if she'll be inclined to speak to you, but we serve tea between four and four thirty and she's in the dining room. You can't miss her. She is the only one with purple hair."

"Thanks, Colin," I said as I took Kyle's hand and led him toward the dining area. Luckily for us, Mrs. Bristow was sitting at a table by herself.

"Mrs. Bristow," I said. She looked up but didn't reply, so I continued. "My name is Tj and this is Kyle. First off, we'd like to offer our condolences for the death of your husband."

"Ex-husband," the woman corrected. "And no need for condolences. I couldn't be happier."

"I see." I glanced at Kyle. He lifted a brow but didn't speak.

"I know that sounds cold, but Striker was a real bastard," Mrs. Bristow continued. "He took all sorts of joy in withholding the support he owed me so I'd have to come begging every month like a dog groveling for scraps. Now that the idiot is dead, I'm a very wealthy woman who will never have to grovel another day in my life. Was there something you wanted?"

"Actually, yes," I answered. "Is it okay if we sit down?"

"It's a public dining room, so I guess it isn't up to me."

I looked at Kyle and shrugged. We both took a seat.

"We apologize for bothering you at teatime, but a friend of ours, Gina Roberts, is missing. We believe she was with your ex-husband when he was shot. We're talking to everyone who may have known what was going on in Mr. Bristow's life to try to figure out what became of her."

"Was your friend Striker's lover?" Mrs. Bristow asked.

"No. She worked for him as a consultant," I replied.

"Hmph."

I could see Mrs. Bristow didn't believe Gina wasn't sleeping with her ex and there was no reason to try to convince her otherwise, so I moved on. "Would you mind telling me when you last saw your ex?"

"Yesterday. I came to town to collect my money, but Striker had been dragging his feet all week. Finally, I'd had enough, so I tracked him down and made it clear I wasn't leaving without the entire amount he owed me."

"About what time was that?"

Mrs. Bristow picked up a delicate tea cake and took a small bite. "I went to his office just before tea. I caught him just as he was preparing to go out. I demanded my money, and much to my surprise, he wrote me a check and even apologized for being late."

"And that was unusual?"

"Damn right. As I said, he used to take all kinds of joy in making me grovel."

"Why do you think he gave in so easily yesterday after putting you off all week?" I asked.

"I imagine he was anxious to be off to wherever it was he was going."

"Was he alone?" I asked.

"He was." The woman glanced at Kyle. "I don't suppose you'd be a dear and see if you can find some brandy for my tea?"

I nodded, and Kyle headed to the bar.

"Ever since Mr. Bristow came to Serenity I've wondered why he chose our town for his project. His résumé suggests he's done much larger projects in much larger cities that I would assume made him a lot more money."

Mrs. Bristow ran her hand over her purple hair and tucked

a strand behind her ear. She took a moment to study me before beginning to speak in a strong voice that left little doubt she had serious feelings about what she was saying. "Striker liked money as well as anyone, I suppose, but it wasn't the driving force in his life. Striker lived for two things: He liked a challenge and he liked to win. When he first came to Paradise Lake he was told by several people, including the mayor, that his project would never fly. People said Serenity was a small town intent on maintaining a small-town feel. They told him he was wasting his time and had best move on. By the end of his first visit here, he was hooked. In his mind, a challenge had been presented and accepted. He would have spent every dime he had if need be to ensure victory. Striker never backed down from a challenge and he didn't like to lose. Not ever."

"So he wanted to build here because the town didn't want him?" I asked.

"Exactly. If your town council had shown interest in his project, he might have realized it wouldn't be a moneymaker and moved on. But once the challenge was issued, he was committed to the fight, and when Striker engaged, he was committed to fighting to the death."

I sat back in the chair and considered the woman across from me. "Do you think that's what happened? Do you think he challenged someone to a fight and lost?"

She shrugged. "Perhaps. Although Striker's choice of weapon wouldn't have been a gun. It would have been much more personal. If he considered you his enemy, he would have figured out what you loved and taken it from you."

"Wow." I couldn't understand why Gina had helped this man. He sounded like a monster. Gina was a smart woman. She must have seen that. "Do you have any idea where he was going yesterday?"

"No. I didn't ask, mostly because I didn't care." Mrs. Bristow looked up as Kyle returned with her brandy. "Why, thank you, dear. Tea without brandy really is just colored water."

Kyle handed the glass to her and retook his chair next to me.

"Is there anything at all you can think of that might help us locate our friend?" I asked. "Anything at all?"

Mrs. Bristow poured the brandy into her tea. "When Striker left his office yesterday he had his own car. From what I understand, his body was found in your friend's. It seems to me if you found Striker's car it might tell you quite a lot about where he went after we spoke."

"Does the car have an emergency response system?" Kyle asked.

"Of course, dear. Nothing but the best for the idiot I married."

Kyle looked at me. "As long as the system hasn't been disabled, we should be able to find out where the car is now." He looked at Mrs. Bristow. "Thank you."

"Happy to help. I do hope your friend is all right."

After we left the inn, Kyle headed back to his place. He had a connection at the DMV who could help us activate the emergency response system in Striker's car. For the first time since Kate had told us Gina was missing, I felt we were on the tracks of a real clue.

Kyle headed to his computer room as soon as we arrived, and I took the dogs out for a quick run. It was after five and we hadn't eaten since breakfast. Maybe once I got back to the house I'd look for something to make for dinner. I assumed it would take Kyle a long time to get the information he needed. I was wrong.

"Bristow's car is at the marina," Kyle said when I entered through the kitchen.

"The marina? Which marina?"

"The one on the east shore. Let's feed the dogs, then go check it out. We'll grab some dinner while we're out."

The East Shore Marina was about a twenty-minute drive from Kyle's place. By the time we'd fed the dogs and made the trip, it was almost six. The car Kyle had identified as belonging to Bristow was parked in a legal parking spot. It was locked and looked as if it hadn't been tampered with.

"If his car is here he must either have met someone who arrived on a boat or rented a boat," I suggested.

"Let's go up to the office and ask. If he rented a boat, they should have a record of the transaction."

It was a Friday in summer and visitors who'd been out on the lake all day were coming in for the evening, so the launchpad and the office were busy. I managed to find a young employee who'd worked the previous day, but he'd been so busy he hadn't noticed who'd driven the vehicle or when it had arrived. He'd notice it was still in the lot when he'd arrived for work that morning and was planning to have it towed because there was a twenty-four-hour parking limit.

I called Roy. I figured he had the power to make sure the car wasn't simply towed away. He said Kate was with him, so we should make ourselves scarce. He was going to tell her he'd received an anonymous tip about the car and promised to stop by Kyle's house when he had a chance to fill us in.

We decided we'd done all we could for the moment, so we drove back to town for a burger and fries. After that we hoped we'd hear from Roy and take things from there. I couldn't have anticipated that what appeared to be our biggest break would be something we stumbled across while we ate dinner at Murphy's.

The pub was crowded, but we managed to find a table near the back. We each ordered a beer and a burger and then sat back to wait for our food to arrive. By this point I was starving and hoped it would come quickly, though with this crowd I sort of doubted it. Another teacher at the high school, Alyson Leery, stopped by our table to ask about Gina. It seemed Kate had told the group at the bonfire just enough to engage their curiosity, but not enough to explain anything.

"Awesome bonfire last night," Alyson commented. At twenty-four, she was our youngest staff member. She'd done her student teaching with Gina last year and had been hired for the upcoming year to teach basic freshman and sophomore math classes.

"It was a beautiful night," I agreed.

"So what exactly is going on with Gina? The new deputy said she was looking for her. She isn't in some sort of trouble, is she?"

"I think Deputy Baldwin just wants to talk to Gina, but she hasn't been able to find her. You haven't seen or spoken to her, have you?"

Alyson shook her head. "Not since yesterday morning at the wakeboarding competition. We only spoke for a minute, but she looked pretty haggard. I figured she didn't show last night because she was sick, but the deputy said she wasn't at her house."

"I checked later and she wasn't there. I'll admit to being a bit worried about her. Did anyone in the crowd last night say they'd seen or spoken to her after she got off volunteer duty yesterday?"

Alyson paused. "You might want to talk to Rick. He started to tell us about a call he got and then everyone got distracted by the lights."

"Lights?" I asked.

"The lights on the lake. Maybe it was after you left. It looked like they were coming from the island. You know, that island is supposed to be haunted."

"Yeah, I've heard the legend." I didn't necessarily believe in ghosts, but it was true that a lot of odd things had occurred on the island in the twenty years since its only resident, Amelia Rosenberg, died under mysterious circumstances. Amelia was an heiress who'd moved to the island after her parents passed away. For reasons unknown to me, she became a total recluse who rarely left the island, choosing to live in isolation until the day she died. The shadowy woman had left a mysterious legacy that served as the basis of a local legend that was shared around campfires to this day.

"Anyway," Alyson continued, "after we saw the lights, the topic of conversation drifted away from Gina, and I don't remember if Rick ever did finish what he'd been about to say."

Rick Tolley was another physical education teacher and the varsity football coach. He and Gina had dated from time to time, but I never had the impression it was anything serious.

"Maybe I'll call him," I said.

"I hope Gina's okay. Ask her to call me once you track her

down. Now I'm worried something bad might have happened to her."

"I'll have her call you once I catch up with her, and thanks again for the information about Rick."

A waitress brought our food and Alyson went back to the table where her friends were eating and sharing a pitcher of beer.

"What do you think?" I asked Kyle after I'd taken the first bite of my hamburger, chewed it, and swallowed.

"I think maybe you should call Rick."

"I plan to," I said after taking a sip of my beer. "But it's the lights on the island that most interest me."

"The lights on the island?" Kyle asked.

"I saw them too. Remember when we were talking before Kate showed up? Rosenberg Island has been uninhabited for twenty years. Occasionally, a boat will dock there and someone will take a look around, but it was late when I saw the lights and completely dark otherwise. It didn't make sense that there would be day trippers on the island, and with all the ghost talk, no one ever camps there."

"So you think there might be a link between the lights and what's going on with Gina?"

I nodded. "Bristow's car was found in the parking lot of the marina closest to the island. By the time I saw the lights, Bristow's body had already been found in Gina's car, but what if he'd been on the island earlier in the day? That would explain why his car was at the marina. What if whoever he was with shot him and somehow Gina got involved and tried to help him? We've pretty much decided Gina was most likely kidnapped by whoever she struggled with near the scene of the car accident.

What if they took her back to the island? It's as good a place as any to hide someone. What if she's still there?"

Kyle frowned. "I suppose that's a viable theory."

"We need to check out the island. Let's finish eating and then grab your boat," I suggested. "I know it will be getting dark by the time we get there and docking on the island is tricky even in the daylight, but your boat has lights and there's no way I can wait until morning to see if Gina is being held there."

"Okay, we'll go, but we're going to tell Roy what we're doing. Maybe he can come along as well. If Gina's being held there, we can assume there's someone else on the island too." Kyle paused, then continued. "In case there are guards on the island, I think we should wait until it's completely dark to make our approach. I can anchor offshore and we can use the dinghy to land on the island. We'll have a better chance of going undetected if there are no lights or sounds from the boat's engine."

"That's a good idea." I looked at the clock on the wall. It was almost seven thirty. "The sun will be down in an hour, and it should be dark enough to avoid detection by nine. Let's finish eating and I'll call Roy."

"Do you have warm clothing at my place? It might be chilly on the water after dark."

"I have a sweatshirt and jeans in my bag. I'd planned to stay the entire weekend, so I came prepared."

I called Roy, who agreed to meet us at Kyle's in thirty minutes. We finished our burgers but left the beer. We didn't know what we'd encounter and didn't want to be impaired in any way. We arrived at Kyle's ahead of Roy, so I took the dogs out while Kyle got the boat fueled and ready to go.

CHAPTER 10

When Roy showed up with guns strapped to most parts of his body, I began to panic. What was I thinking? I was a high school teacher responsible for raising my two young sisters, not James Bond. The sight of Roy all decked out in his vest and weapons brought home the potential danger of the situation.

"Here's how it's going to go," Roy said after he handed over Gina's computer to Kyle but before we boarded the boat. "We're going to the island in a recon capacity only. If there are individuals on the island who appear to be armed, we'll call Kate to request backup. We'll watch from a distance until backup arrives, but we won't in any way approach anyone who even looks like they might be armed."

"Agreed," Kyle said.

"Yeah, okay," I seconded.

Roy continued. "I considered calling Kate before I came over here, but it's most likely the lights you saw were just kids partying, and I didn't want to alert her to the fact that we're working together if I don't have to—although she's a smart woman and probably already suspects something like this."

Roy was right. Once he came back, it made sense she'd realize we'd been talking to him. For some reason she hadn't made an issue of it yet.

"If there's someone on the island, will they be able to see the boat's lights from the cove where you plan to anchor?" Roy asked Kyle.

"No, there's a hill between the cove and the part of the lake where the island is located."

"That's good. If there's anyone there, we'll need to sneak up on them if we want to avoid engagement."

Roy went over a few additional procedural and safety items while Kyle prepared to depart. By the time we left the dock it was almost dark. Kyle used his lights as well as his instruments to navigate a safe path to the cove where he'd decided to anchor and transfer to the dinghy.

Roy sat in the front of the dinghy with me in the middle and Kyle in the back. The small boat had a motor, but we wanted to arrive on the island undetected, so we rowed quietly toward the mouth of the cove as the sky darkened completely and the stars began to shine in the night sky.

"That's the island just ahead," I said in a soft voice. "It's probably about a half mile from here."

"I don't see any lights," Kyle replied.

"Yeah." I felt my hope fade. "Me neither."

"Let's continue and look around," Roy said. "Even if no one is there now, there may be clues left behind if someone was there last night."

Kyle, Roy, and I settled into a steady rowing pattern as we neared the backside of the island. I'd been so hopeful that we'd find Gina. It had been almost twenty-four hours since I'd learned she was missing, but it felt like days. God, I was tired.

"If a boat were to dock on the island it would be on the east side," Roy said. "There's only a narrow strip where the rocks can be navigated. We can maneuver around the rocks with the dinghy, so I suggest we tie up on the west side and then make our way around the island by foot."

We agreed with him and quietly and carefully tied up the dinghy and started around the island, hugging the beach as we did. I hadn't seen any lights or heard anything, but I was still hopeful there would be clues to be found. When we were almost exactly halfway around the island, Roy held up his hand. We'd been walking around him but now paused.

"Do you see anything?" I whispered in Roy's ear.

"Maybe." He turned around. "The two of you wait here. I'm going to check it out."

"But..."

Roy gave me a hard look. "Wait here. That's the deal."

I nodded, and Roy headed inland. There was a large rock nearby, so I took a seat. After a minute, Kyle joined me.

"What do you think he saw?" I whispered.

"I don't know. I didn't see or hear anything."

"It's so quiet. There's no way Gina's here."

Kyle put his arm around my shoulders and gave me a squeeze. "We'll find her."

"In time?"

Kyle didn't answer. He was a smart man and I was sure he realized, as I did, that with every minute that passed, the chance we'd find Gina alive diminished.

I looked out over the calm water. The moon had begun to rise over the distant mountain, creating a trail of light in the inky darkness. I felt so lost and alone, even though I knew Kyle was doing everything he could to keep my hopes up. *Where are you, Gina?*

"What's that sound?" Kyle asked after a few minutes went by.

I listened carefully. At first I didn't hear anything, but after listening hard, I realized I was hearing a strange tapping. "I don't know," I whispered back.

"I thought it might be a tree branch hitting against something, but there's literally no wind," Kyle replied.

"It could be a bird, though most birds aren't out after dark."

"Maybe it's a squirrel up a tree, trying to dislodge a pinecone?" Kyle suggested.

I listened again, but the sound seemed to have stopped. I waited for it to return. Now the only sound I could hear was my own breath. "I wonder what's taking Roy so long," I said after another minute. "It seems he should know by now whether or not we're alone."

"I imagine he's taking his time. If there's anyone on the island, I'm sure he doesn't want to alert them to our presence."

I closed my eyes and laid my head on Kyle's shoulder. It seemed like Roy had been gone for hours, even though I knew that couldn't be true. I was beginning to nod off when I heard the tapping again. I sat up straight. "Did you hear that?"

"I heard it. It sounds like it's coming from farther inland."

"Maybe we should check it out," I said.

"Roy told us to wait here."

I was about to argue when Roy came toward us from down the beach. He had his flashlight on, so he must be fairly certain we were alone.

"Did you find anything?" I asked.

"It doesn't appear anyone is here now, but someone has

been here recently. Not only are there a ton of fresh footprints on the beach but I found beer cans, chip bags, and candy wrappers floating in the water near the small dock. If I had to guess, the lights you saw last night were teens partying."

"So Gina probably wasn't here last night," I concluded.

"It looks that way, but I did find this." Roy held up a phone with a Serenity High School phone cover.

"That could be Gina's phone," I said. "She has a cover like that, although a lot of people have the same one. Does the phone work?"

"I found it in the water near the shore. It's completely drenched and inoperable. If this is Gina's phone, that would explain why your calls have been going directly to voicemail. I'll take it back with me to see if someone can pull up ownership information from it. Even if it turns out it's Gina's phone though, I'm not sure it will help us find her. She may have been here at one time, but she isn't here now."

"I'm guessing she wasn't here when the party was going on, but she might have been here earlier in the day," I suggested.

"What makes you think that?" Roy asked.

"Maybe she met Bristow at the marina and came out to the island with him for some reason. Maybe he wasn't satisfied just with ruining Serenity with his strip mall. Maybe he wanted to develop this island as well."

"Doubtful," Roy responded.

"Yeah, I know," I admitted. "I guess I'm just grasping at straws. None of this makes sense. Even if Gina and Bristow did come out to the island for some reason, how did he end up in Gina's car? Why not take his own back to town after the trip to the island?"

"Maybe his wouldn't start and they decided to take hers to wherever they were going next," Kyle suggested.

"Did you tow Bristow's car?" I asked Roy.

"Yes," Roy confirmed.

"Can you find out if it's operable?"

"I'll check in the morning. If it won't start, I guess we can assume that's why Gina and Bristow began using her car after leaving the marina. We should head back."

"Why not look around some more?" I asked. "There may be other clues."

"I looked around as best I could, but it's dark, and the interior of the island is fairly dense with foliage," Roy answered. "Maybe we can come back when it's light."

"Did you look inside the stone house Amelia lived in?" I asked.

"It's boarded up and doesn't look as if it's been disturbed."

"What about the strange noise?" I asked.

"What noise?" Roy asked.

"Listen. It's a sort of a tapping sound."

Everyone fell into silence.

"See. Right there," I said. "Did you hear it?"

"I'm pretty sure that's the old pump. It's an ancient device that draws water from the lake. I noticed a ticking sound coming from it when I checked the house. I suppose—" Roy was interrupted by the ringing of his phone. He took it out of his pocket and answered. He listened for a moment, then replied, "Okay, I'll be there as soon as I can." Roy looked at us. "I need to go. There's been a new development and Kate wants me to come in." Roy looked at Kyle. "The outboard motor on the dinghy does work?"

"It works. We just didn't want the noise as we approached. If being quiet isn't an issue, I can have you back to your car in thirty minutes."

"Let's go."

We'd boarded the dinghy and Kyle had started back toward his boat before I looked at Roy. "What development?"

"I don't know, Kate didn't say. She just asked if I could meet her at the office."

"It's pretty late and you've both put in a ton of hours. It must be something pretty significant for her not to just wait until morning."

"I got the feeling she had big news she didn't want to discuss on the phone," Roy confirmed.

"You'll call me once you know what it is?"

Roy didn't respond right away. At last he nodded.

When we arrived back at Kyle's, Roy left immediately, and I helped Kyle tie up and cover the boat.

"You should think about putting in a lift," I said as we made sure the boat was tucked in tight enough to weather a strong wind should one come up.

"I've been thinking about building a boat house, but I'd need to move it around the cove a bit. I wouldn't want to obstruct the view of the water from the house."

"I'm sure if there isn't a deep enough channel to move the docking location, you could have one dredged."

"I could. But that would be a big project. For now, the exterior dock is working fine."

I followed Kyle up the walkway to the house. The dogs acted like we'd been gone for years instead of just a couple of hours. Despite the fact that I was exhausted, I was wound up. Kyle wanted to check on the program he'd left running on the computer, which he hoped could unlock the secure file in Gina's account, and I decided to take the dogs for a quick walk. I was super curious about what Kate wanted to discuss with Roy and hoped he'd call before turning in for the night. Of course, I was so tried I'd most likely sleep right through the ringing of my phone if he didn't call before we turned in. I took my phone from my pocket with the idea of turning up the volume. When I clicked on it, I noticed I had a message from Hunter.

"Hey, Tj. I just wanted to let you know I got back the DNA results from Gina and the man who's staying in her house. There's no way they're related. Given the situation, I called the sheriff's office and spoke to Deputy Baldwin. I thought the DNA results for Gina's mysterious visitor might shed some light on what's going on if she can find a match. It's about ten o'clock. I should be up until around eleven thirty. If you get this message and have any questions, feel free to call."

I looked at the clock. It was ten minutes after eleven. I hit Return Call and waited.

"I see you got my message," Hunter answered.

"I did. I'm sorry it took so long. My ringer must have been off. So Gina was right: the man she's been sharing her home with isn't who he claims to be."

"Even when you factor in the half-sibling scenario, there's no way they're related. When I spoke to Deputy Baldwin, she seemed pretty excited that I got DNA results so quickly. She's going to try to find a match."

"Can she do that? Can DNA give you the name of the person it was harvested from?"

"Not necessarily. If a piece of evidence is found that

contains DNA, the results from the test Gina asked me to run would prove whether the DNA belonged to the man in question. And there's a federal database that has samples from some individuals, including those with recent criminal convictions, which can sometimes provide a match. It's a long shot, but it could provide a piece of the puzzle. All I know at this point is that the odds are extremely low that this man is Gina's biological brother. So low I wouldn't even consider it to be a possibility."

"He has to be involved in whatever's going on. Thank you, Hunter. Maybe if we can figure out who he is, we can figure out where Gina is."

"I hope it helps. Like I said before, feel free to call if there's anything else I can do to help make sure Gina gets home safe and sound."

"You're a good guy, Hunter."

I hung up and started back to the house. The new lead Kate had called Roy about must have to do with the DNA test. Maybe she already had a match.

When I arrived in Kyle's office, he was staring at the computer screen. "Something wrong?" I asked in response to the frown on his face.

"I got into the file."

I smiled. "That's wonderful. What was in it?"

"Numbers."

"What kind of numbers?"

"There appear to be eight sets of numbers with four numbers in each set. It must be a code or key of some sort."

"A key? What kind of key?"

Kyle didn't answer. I walked over to peer over his shoulder. As he had said, the only thing in the file were columns of numbers. "What do we do with this?"

"I'm not sure. I need some time to study the numbers. Maybe I can find a pattern."

"I'll make us some coffee."

I made the coffee and gave a cup to Kyle, then sat down on the sofa in his office. I took a few sips of coffee, then leaned my head back to rest my eyes while I waited for it to do its job.

CHAPTER 11

Saturday, August 12

I woke the next morning wrapped in Kyle's arms. His warm breath caressed my cheek as he snored softly. I took a moment to enjoy the perfection of the moment, even though we were both fully dressed and lying on top of the covers in his bed. Talk about irony. I had been dreaming for weeks about waking up in Kyle's arms for the first time. I'd just figured it would be after we'd finally taken the next step in our relationship.

Once again, I didn't remember coming into the bedroom, so Kyle must have carried me in after I'd fallen asleep. If I knew him, he'd probably worked into the wee hours of the morning. The poor guy must be exhausted. I didn't want to wake him, so I carefully unwound his arms from around my body and tiptoed into the kitchen.

I put on a pot of coffee before slipping into my tennis shoes and sweatshirt and taking the dogs out for their morning run. It was a beautiful morning. The sky was just beginning to turn light, although the sun had yet to make an appearance over the distant mountain peak. The air was still and the water calm as I walked along the sandy shore. Echo and Trooper were thoroughly enjoying their early morning romp, running side by side carrying the same long stick.

Roy never had called last night unless it was after I'd fallen asleep. I hated to call him so early, so I was going to have to employ some of the patience I was always telling Ashley and Gracie they needed to have and wait until the rest of the world awakened before getting the answers I was dying for.

As I walked along the sandy beach, I tried to get my head around the things we'd been able to uncover so far. We knew Striker Bristow had been shot in the back and that he'd eventually ended up strapped into Gina's car, which had ended up in a field wrapped around a tree. We knew Gina had been working with Bristow on his new proposal, and Bristow wasn't popular among many of the locals.

We suspected Gina had been driving the vehicle in which Bristow's body had been found, and that she had been pursued at the crash site and eventually forced into another car. Additionally, we suspected she was being held by someone associated with Bristow, but we didn't know who or even why.

As far as I knew, there hadn't been any ransom demands. Bristow was dead. What more could anyone want from Gina?

I was bothered by the fact the man who'd claimed to be her long-lost brother wasn't, yet he still had been staying in her house all week. Who was he and how did he fit into things?

And then there was the fact that Bristow's car had been found at the marina and a phone that might be Gina's had been found on Rosenberg Island. What on earth could the island have to do with any of this?

Right now, there were as many possible theories as there

were variables. We needed to figure out a way to narrow things down. Gina had been missing for thirty-six hours. Surely if she were still alive, time was running out.

I called the dogs back and turned back to the house. When I arrived, I went upstairs. The bed was empty, but it sounded like Kyle was in the shower. I was tempted to join him but suddenly felt shy and uncertain, so I headed back downstairs and started breakfast.

"How long have you been up?" Kyle asked when he walked across the room to deliver a quick kiss on my lips as I spooned scrambled eggs onto a platter.

"About an hour. I took the dogs for a quick run and then attempted to make breakfast without burning it."

"It looks good."

I smiled. "I'm rather proud of myself. Even the toast is golden brown. What time did you come to bed?"

"Not that long after you fell asleep. I tried to work longer, but I pretty much hit a wall and my mind refused to work. Have you heard from Roy?"

"Not yet. If he doesn't call by nine, I'll call him. I hate to call earlier, I have no idea how late he worked last night. So, no luck figuring out what the number sequences mean?"

"Not yet. I'll take another look after we eat. A few hours' sleep can do wonders for your concentration."

I took a bite of my egg. It was actually light and fluffy. Maybe I had finally outgrown the cooking curse I had lived under for most of my life, which pretty much assured that anything I made was overdone, underdone, too salty, or tasteless.

"Other than trying to figure out what the numbers in the

file mean, where are we with our current plan of action?" I asked.

Kyle took a sip of his coffee, then sat back in his chair. "There are two people on our list we haven't spoken to yet: Clint Buford, who was suing Bristow for not paying him for the plans he chose not to use; and Rick Tolley, the PE teacher at the high school who was interrupted while telling the gang about a call he received."

"What about the emails between Gina and Carter Kline?" I asked. "Maybe we should try to figure out who he is."

"I'll do that once I'm done with the numbers."

"Okay. I'll call Roy while you do that. And I feel like someone should go back to the island in the daylight and take another look around."

"I wouldn't mind making the trip out there after I take another stab at the numbers."

"I'll call Roy and Rick while you work on the number sequences. I don't know Clint Buford, so it might be best if you spoke to him or we spoke to him together."

After breakfast Kyle returned to his computer and I tidied up the kitchen. When I was done, I logged onto my contact list to see if I had a cell number for Rick. Unfortunately, I didn't. Rick and I were members of the same department but not really friends outside of work. I figured Greg Remington would have his number, so I called him instead.

"Hi Greg, it's Tj," I said when he answered.

"Tj, I'm glad you called. Have you heard from Gina?"

"No, I'm afraid not. I called because Alyson Leery told me that Rick Tolley was telling the group at the bonfire about a phone call he'd received that had something to do with Gina but was interrupted. I thought I'd follow up with him to see if it's anything relevant, but I don't have his number. I hoped you did and wouldn't mind giving it to me."

"I have it, but I shouldn't give out staff numbers. How about I call him, give him your number, and ask him to call you?"

"That would be fine. Listen, while I have you, I spoke briefly to Sheila about the project Gina worked on last spring. She didn't have a lot of details, but with Gina missing, I thought it might be important to know what the project entailed."

Greg hesitated before answering. "I don't have all the details myself. I just know she was asked to join the project to help with the mathematics involved. In addition to Gina, an astrophysicist, an engineer, and some others were asked to participate. I think there were six people total in the group."

"Do you know who was behind the project? Was it private sector? Military? Government?"

"I'm not sure. Gina didn't say. I do know it was referred to as SCABS."

The file in Gina's online storage. The over-the-top security made sense now. "Thanks, Greg. If you hear from Gina, please let me know."

"I will. And I'll ask that you do the same."

Next, I called Roy. It wasn't quite nine o'clock yet, but I was getting impatient. I knew in my gut that today had to be the day we found Gina if we had any chance of finding her alive. Of course, she might not even be injured. She might simply be a well-cared-for captive. Or at least I hoped that was the case.

Roy answered on the first ring and didn't sound groggy or irritated in the least.

"Sorry I didn't call you last night," Roy jumped right in. "I was with Kate until almost two a.m. and figured you'd have gone to bed by then. Besides, I was exhausted and needed a few hours of sleep while I could get it."

"No problem. What was the big news she wanted to share with you?"

"Had you heard that Gina had asked Hunter to run her DNA against her brother's?"

"Yes, I had. Hunter told me it wasn't a match. Was that Kate's big news?"

"Not exactly."

I waited, but Roy didn't continue. "Okay, so what exactly? Did you find a match for the guy claiming to be Spencer?"

"Not yet. Kate has a buddy in the FBI who's agreed to use the federal database to do a search. Kate called me in because she went out to the accident site for a second look. She found a handheld radio in the shrubbery near where it appears a struggle occurred. When Kate first found it, she couldn't hear a thing on it, so she tossed it in the tray on the dash of her squad car. She was driving around last night out on County Road 47, near the old dam. She heard a strange sound and realized it was static. She traveled a bit further, and picked up voices, but shortly after, the radio went dead."

"If she heard voices, could she tell what they were saying?"

"No. There was too much static."

"So why did the radio go dead?"

"Kate wasn't sure if someone had realized a connection had been established and the device was turned off, or if whoever was on the other end was on the move and was out of range. Kate and I drove around last night trying to pick up the signal, but we didn't have any luck. Listen, Kate just pulled up, so I have to go. I'll call you back when I can."

"Wait. Did you find out if Bristow's car works?"

"It does," Roy confirmed, "so we have no idea why he left it at the marina. I gotta go."

I glared at the phone. I hated feeling so helpless while my friend was most likely suffering at the hands of whoever had shot Bristow. Sitting around waiting for the phone to ring didn't work for me, but I didn't want to pull Kyle away from the computer. I needed to come up with something I could do on my own. I'd promised Grandpa I'd help at the resort this afternoon. After my dad's accident, we'd cut back quite a bit on the events Maggie's Hideaway would sponsor for this year's Summer Festival, but Grandpa had wanted to do something because the resort had been part of the festival since its very first year. We'd ultimately decided to host the beach volleyball tournament, a bands on the beach, and a hamburger cook-off on Saturday night.

It was 9:20 now and I didn't need to be at the resort until three. I desperately needed a shower and I should check in with the staff, so maybe I'd head to the resort, get cleaned up there and check in, and then go into town to see if I could find anyone who might have seen or spoken to Gina in the days before her disappearance.

I was sitting on the front deck and was about to go inside to discuss my plans with Kyle when my phone rang.

"Hey, Rick. Did Greg tell you why I wanted to speak to you?"

"He said you're still looking for Gina and wanted to know what I was going to share with the group before I was interrupted."

"Exactly. Do you remember what you were about to say?"

"I was telling the group I'd talked to Gina on the phone that afternoon. She'd called me to ask if she could borrow the satellite phone I use when I go backpacking."

"Satellite phone?"

"She wanted to use it to test something, or maybe to confirm something. I'm not exactly sure. You know Gina's always tinkering with one idea or another."

"Am I right in thinking a satellite phone will work just about anywhere?"

"Pretty much. There are limitations, of course. It won't work underground or if the satellite signal is blocked by a cliff or some other solid object that's between the phone and the satellite, but it can be a godsend when you're in the backcountry away from cell service and you have an accident."

"Did you lend it to her?" I asked.

"I told her I'd be happy to lend it to her, but I was out on the water in the middle of a sailing date. I was about to head back, so I asked if she could come by to pick it up at around five thirty. She said she would, but she never did."

"Did she say anything else that might give me a clue as to where she was or where she was going?"

"I don't know where she was specifically, but I could hear the loudspeaker in the background announcing the finalists for the bake-off."

"Which was held at the community center. Do you remember what time you spoke to her?"

"I guess it must have been around four. I hope you find her. When the new deputy said she was looking for her, I didn't think anything of it, but now..."

"Yeah, I'm worried too. If you hear from her or talk to anyone who has, please let me know."

"I will."

After I hung up, I was about to go inside to talk to Kyle when my phone rang again.

"Hey, Grandpa. Did you think of something you needed me to do?"

"After I spoke to you, Sterling Snow called," my grandfather said, referring to the owner of Angel Mountain, the third-largest ski area at the lake and the largest on the north shore.

"What did he want?" I asked.

"To set up a meeting to talk to your dad about Winter Carnival. I know your dad said to call Rosalie's phone if we needed anything because he'd be tied up most of the time they were away, but I couldn't remember her number."

"Winter Carnival isn't for six months. Can't it wait?"

"That's what I wondered," Grandpa said. "But Sterling said his father was all up in arms about something and insisting the planning had to begin immediately."

Sterling's father, Bradford, had built the resort from the ground up in the same way my grandfather had built Maggie's Hideaway. And my dad had taken over when Grandpa retired, just as Sterling had taken over from his father. The senior Mr. Snow had a reputation for being somewhat high-strung, and I imagined he'd been badgering Sterling relentlessly to get moving on what was most likely their largest income producer of the year.

"I'll give you Rosalie's number, but there's nothing Dad can do until he gets back from Sacramento. I'll call Sterling to explain the situation if you want."

"No, I can do it. I don't even know why I bothered you. It's just Sterling tends to go a bit overboard when it comes to making sure his dad is happy."

"Yeah, those two have a complicated relationship."

"I'll write down Rosalie's number in case of emergencies, but I'll handle it for now. I'll see you this afternoon."

"Actually, I'll be coming by the resort to shower and change soon. We can talk about it some more when I get there."

"Okay, sweetheart. I'll see you in a while."

I hung up and once again started back into the house. I still didn't have my car, but Kyle had several vehicles, so I didn't think he'd mind if I borrowed his truck. My new plan was to go into town to see who'd been at the bake-off on Thursday afternoon after I stopped at the resort to get cleaned up. If I could fill the holes in my timeline, I might finally be able to make sense of things.

CHAPTER 12

"Did you get Sterling handled?" I asked Grandpa after I'd showered and then tracked him down in the lodge. The resort was busy, as it usually was during the summer, and Grandpa liked to make the rounds and check to make sure everything was running smoothly.

"I did. I told him that I'd leave a message for Mike to call him when he got back into town, but I wasn't going to bother him before that."

"How did he take the news?" I asked.

"Not well, but he seemed to understand that there wasn't a lot anyone could do until Mike returned. I did promise to pull some data he wanted relating to past events. I think that pacified him a bit."

"I'm glad you managed to talk him down. How are things going otherwise?"

"Fine. The resort is booked solid, but the staff seems to have a handle on things. In fact, all I've really been doing is wandering around, bothering everyone."

I couldn't help but smile. "I'm sure you're doing more than that. I still plan to be here by three for the volleyball tournament. I think Kyle plans to help out as well. Do you need me to do anything at all between now and then?"

"I think we're good. Noah is making sure all the contestants for the hamburger cook-off have what they need, and the marina staff have taken care of putting up the nets for the volleyball tournament." Noah was our new general manager. He normally worked directly under my father, but since Dad had been laid up Noah'd taken on a much larger role. "Although we're running low on rum for our frozen rum punch," Grandpa said. "If you wouldn't mind picking some up, that would help quite a lot."

"Do you need it before three?"

"No. Just bring it when you come for the tournament."

"Okay, great. Have you checked in with the ice cream parlor yet? They tend to run low when it's as hot out as it is today."

Maggie's Hideaway was a large inclusive resort that required a lot of oversight. Not only did we have a marina, an ice cream shop, a sports rental shop, a stable, lodgings that included a campground, an inn, a lodge, and individual cabins, but we also had the Lakeside Bar and Grill, so the guests never had to leave the resort.

"I called our supplier and I'm having more ice cream delivered this afternoon. I know that more often than not, things we weren't counting on come up, but I think with the exception of the rum, we should be fine for the weekend."

"Okay. I'll see you this afternoon. If you need me before that, call me."

I decided to head into town to try to figure out who may have seen Gina when she was within hearing range of the bake-off on Thursday. The event had been held at the community center where something different was scheduled for each afternoon during the festival. Rick had said he'd spoken to Gina at around four that day, which meant it was after Gina and Bristow had eaten together at lunchtime. I knew Mrs. Bristow had confronted her ex-husband in his office at around that same time, so they must have split up after lunch, then met up again later.

It was just before eleven when I arrived at the community center. Today's event was a quilt show. As they were every year, the quilts that had been entered were breathtaking. I wished I had time to look around, but I was determined to find Gina before the sun set on another day.

Inside the crowded building, I looked around for someone who might have been here on Thursday. My eyes settled on Frannie Edison, the local librarian, who I was sure had volunteered all four afternoons. Frannie was an extremely nice if somewhat conservative woman who'd never married or had children but loved the library and the town as if it were her family.

"Morning, Frannie," I called out.

"Tj! I didn't expect to see you today. Are you here to help out?"

"I'm afraid not. I'm looking for someone who was here for the bake-off on Thursday."

"I was here," Frannie confirmed. "I'm here all four days for the events here."

"Do you remember seeing Gina Roberts?"

Frannie nodded. "Yes. She was here in the afternoon. She came around the time the judging was wrapping up. She wanted to buy a cake when the entries were released for sale. I think she planned to take it to a meeting she was attending that evening."

"Did she happen to share any details about the meeting?"

"No. She didn't say anything else about it. Why?"

"It just seems like a lot of trouble to go to, to wait around to buy an award-winning cake for a business meeting."

"I suppose she could have been meeting a friend, or even a boyfriend. She didn't say who she was meeting, just that she had a meeting to go to."

"Do you know how long she was here?"

Frannie tapped her chin with her index finger. "The bake-off entries were put up for sale at around four thirty and they were all gone by five, so she must have left at some point during that half hour."

"I've been trying to get hold of her, but she isn't at home and she isn't answering her cell. The last time anyone saw her was Thursday, so I'm looking into where she was and who she was with before she disappeared."

"Disappeared? Is she missing?"

I supposed I could fill Frannie in on the details of the car accident where Striker Bristow's body was found, but I hated to worry her if I didn't have to. "I'm not certain she's missing exactly. I just haven't been able to get hold of her. Did you notice if she was with anyone when she was here?"

Frannie seemed to be considering my question. "I believe she arrived alone, but I did see her chatting with Bree—who'd entered her peach pie—while she waited on the judges."

Bree Henderson was Jenna's sister, who had been filling in at the restaurant while she and Helen were camping with the girls. Bree was single and worked as a nanny for the local pastor's young daughter. She had a friendly manner and a way of knowing everything that was going on with everyone in town. She'd be a good one to talk to. I suspected I'd find her at the

Antiquery at this time of day. The restaurant was open for breakfast and lunch and closed at two, but between six a.m. and two p.m. they were almost always slammed.

When I arrived, I saw Bree working the hostess station. The place was pretty busy, so I'd have to follow her around to chat with her while she sat customers and served drinks.

"Hey, Tj," Bree said. "How are you enjoying your weekend off?"

"So far all I've done is look for Gina. Have you seen her?"

"Gina Roberts?"

I nodded.

"Did something happen to her?"

"I'm not sure."

I watched Bree's face change from curious to concerned as she seemed to consider my question. She was petite with dark curly hair, the complete opposite of tall, blonde Jenna. If you didn't know they were sisters, it would never have occurred to you. "Jenna told me you were on another case, but the reception was bad when we spoke, and we didn't stay on the phone long. I had no idea it involved Gina. What exactly is going on?"

"I can fill you in if you can take a break."

Bree motioned for one of the waitresses to come up to the front to cover for her. Then she led me to the booth Jenna kept in a corner of the kitchen where her daughters did their homework when she had to work late for one reason or another.

"So what's up?" Bree asked. "What happened to Gina?"

I filled her in on the highlights of what we knew to date. I knew she could keep a secret, and I figured Jenna would fill her in anyway if they managed to speak again when the reception was better.

"Wow. I'm so sorry. Poor Gina." Bree narrowed her gaze. "How can I help?"

"I'm trying to map her movements on Thursday. She volunteered at the wakeboarding competition in the morning and then met Striker Bristow for lunch. I know she was at the bake-off where she bought a cake. That was at around five. Roy seems to think the accident occurred sometime between seven and eight. The car was found at eight, anyway. I'm trying to figure out where she went after she left the bake-off."

Bree sat quietly for a moment before answering. "I chatted with her while we waited for the judges to do their thing. I remember her saying she was meeting someone for dinner but wanted to bring a cake to a friend first."

"Did she give you any idea who the friend was, or where the meeting was going to be?"

Bree shook her head. "She didn't say."

"I spoke to Rick Tolley, who told me Gina wanted to borrow a satellite phone from him, then never showed up to pick it up. I don't know why she wanted the phone, but her cell phone isn't working. I've called and called, but it goes right to voice mail."

Bree bit her lower lip. "She may have lost it in the struggle."

"Perhaps. A phone was found on Rosenberg Island that has the same cover as Gina's, but I can't say for certain it's hers. It was in the water, so it doesn't work anymore, but Roy was going to try to trace its ownership. It probably won't turn out to be Gina's, but if she was on the island, I can't figure out the timeline. If she was at the bake-off at five and drove straight to the marina on the east shore, by the time she boarded a boat—assuming there was one waiting for her—she wouldn't have gotten to the island until six. Her car was found at eight. That means Bristow was either shot on the island or at the marina after they returned."

"The marina is a busy place. Someone would have seen it if it happened at the marina, especially at that time of day."

"True. But we found Bristow's car there."

Bree tilted her head. "What if Gina was picked up somewhere else?"

"Go on," I encouraged.

"You said Mrs. Bristow met her ex at around four o'clock. Gina was at the bake-off until around five. What if Bristow drove to the east shore marina, boarded a boat, then picked Gina up somewhere else?"

"Okay, I follow. Bristow and presumably whoever they were meeting picked Gina up somewhere on this end of the lake. They headed out to the island, where Gina lost her phone. After they finished their business there, they dropped Gina off wherever she'd left her car. It must have been at that point that someone shot Bristow and Gina tried to help him get away. The person who shot him could even have been on the boat."

"That's true. You did say he was shot in the back. Maybe he was walking away from the boat when he was shot."

I sat quietly, mulling that over in my head. "Here's where that theory falls apart. If Gina had been picked up somewhere other than the east shore marina and Bristow was shot in the back by someone on the boat, who followed them in a car? There's evidence Gina survived the accident and headed into the woods. If the evidence we found tells the story we think it does, someone accosted her as she tried to get away. We assumed she was followed."

Bree nodded. "Yeah, that part of the story doesn't fit. The

only way it works is if there were two people, or two sets of people: whoever shot Bristow in the back and whoever followed and accosted Gina."

I rubbed my forehead with one hand. "This thing is giving me a headache."

"You look like you haven't slept in days. I understand the urgency, but at some point, you're going to need to let your body replenish itself."

"I'll rest when Gina is found. Not before."

Bree hugged me. "Take care of yourself, Tj. You won't be able to help Gina if you pass out from exhaustion."

"I know you're right, but it's hard to focus on anything but finding Gina."

"I'll be done here by four. If you need anything at all, you have my number."

"Thanks. I may take you up on your offer at some point. And if you hear anything at all that might help us understand what happened to Gina, call me."

"Absolutely. That goes without saying."

I left the Antiquery and headed back to Kyle's house. I really did have a headache, and a few minutes with a wet towel over my eyes seemed like the perfect way to convince it to go away. When I walked in the door, I found Kyle in the kitchen with the two dogs.

Kyle greeted me with a kiss. "You're back sooner than I thought you'd be."

"Headache. I'm going to take some aspirin and regroup. I have some news, but first, did you figure out the numbers from the locked file?"

"Not yet. I have a program working on it. If it's a message

using known encryption methods, the program should figure it out given enough time. If it's something that only makes sense to Gina, I'm not sure we'll be able to figure it out without her. I was about to make a sandwich. Do you want one?"

"Thanks. I'd like that."

Kyle set a sandwich and a glass of milk in front of me and sat down across the table. "What time do we need to be at the resort?"

"We should head over at around three. The volleyball tournament begins at four."

"Maybe after you eat you should take a nap," Kyle suggested.

"I can't sleep knowing Gina could be out there somewhere waiting for someone to rescue her."

Kyle placed his hand over mine. "Yeah, I get that. Let's go over everything again."

"Now that you've had a chance to look at Gina's computer, did you find anything on the hard drive?"

"No. She wiped it before she dropped it off at the repair shop. It was a smart move. You never know who might have access to the hard drive. She may have more than one online storage site. I found another username and password on her cheat sheet that doesn't seem to belong to anything. At least not anything we've found so far."

"They may be associated with a bank account," I said.

"Perhaps."

"Okay, as you suggested before I interrupted, let's go over everything we know so far. We have to be missing something." I took a couple of bites of my sandwich and a couple of sips of milk and then began. "We know Gina was at the wakeboarding contest in the morning and had lunch with Bristow at around one. We aren't sure what Gina and Bristow did after that, but we know he was in his office being yelled at by his ex at around four o'clock and Gina was at the bake-off waiting to buy a cake before five. Kate said they found Gina's car at around eight o'clock, so whatever went south did so between five, when Gina left the bake-off, and when the car was found. I also spoke to Rick, who said he spoke to Gina on the phone around four."

"So what happened between five and eight?"

"I wish I knew."

CHAPTER 13

The resort was totally packed by the time Kyle and I stopped for the rum and delivered it. Luckily, there was parking for the family and our guests at the back of the house because the main parking lot and even the overflow lot were full. Beach volleyball was a popular sport at Paradise Lake. Our soft white sand beach was the perfect venue for it.

The beach volleyball tournament could be entered by anyone who could put together a team of four players. Every year we had some teams that worked together on a regular basis and were really good, and others with members who'd never played together before. It was a single elimination event, so the pool was whittled down to the best teams in fairly short order. Kyle and I had volunteered as judges, so all the games were called fairly. But by the time the final four teams had been set in the semifinals, the sun was dipping behind the mountain. It stayed light fairly late during the long days of summer, but once the sun was down behind the mountain, the air became chilly.

"The smell of the burgers cooking all evening has made me hungry," I said to Grandpa, who came over to check in with me.

"You're free to taste to your heart's content once this set is complete. Any word about Gina?"

"Not yet. If I could think of anything else to do, I'd do it, but it seems like she's just disappeared."

"Are you certain she hasn't left the area of her own volition?"

I pushed my hands into the small of my back to relieve the tension that had been building there. "I don't think so, but at this point I'm not sure of anything. No one I've spoken to has seen or heard from her since Thursday, and Roy told me that Kate has been knocking on doors and chasing even the smallest lead with no luck. My brain is fried. I'm hoping a juicy burger will give me the energy I need to work on things a bit more when we're done here."

"It seems to me the best thing you can do is get a good night's rest. Without it, you're going to crash and burn."

"I know. But trying to rest when I don't know if Gina is injured or not, alive or dead is pretty much impossible."

Grandpa tilted his head of white hair, then lifted one brow, as if he'd just had an idea. "Maybe," he began, "you should talk to Doc and Bookman. If nothing else, it's always a good idea to get a fresh set of eyes on a complicated situation. I can have them meet us up at the house when volleyball is over. I think they should be freed up from helping with the burger judging by then."

That wasn't a bad idea. Grandpa's friend Doc had been a Los Angeles County Medical Examiner for a lot of years before he retired, and Bookman was a mystery writer with a flair for being able to read between the lines.

"I love that idea. If you can set it up with them, I'll find Kyle and let him know what we're doing."

After Grandpa walked away, I returned my attention to the

tournament. I knew I should be focusing on the event, but I found myself distracted. Beach volleyball was a fun sport to both play and watch and normally I was totally into it, but this year all I could think about was Gina and the fact that I wasn't doing more to find her.

"Your dad around?"

I turned around to see Bradford Spalding standing behind me. Bradford had built Angel Mountain, the largest ski resort on the north shore of Paradise Lake, at around the same time my grandpa had built Maggie's Hideaway. Like my grandpa, he was retired, but also like my grandpa, he tended to have a presence in the community as well as at the resort he founded.

"He's in Sacramento this weekend. Can I help you with something?"

"What I have to discuss with your father is important and not something a young'un like you can help me with. When will he be back?"

"Next week. Are you sure I can't help you? I do help out when he is away, you know." Sterling and my grandpa had both been robust hardworking men who claimed the land with their bare hands, but today Sterling looked both old and frail. I guess age was catching up with him.

"Thanks, but I'll wait for your dad."

With that he walked away. Chances were Bradford hadn't spoken to Sterling about the fact that he had already tried to get in contact with my dad. The transition between my grandfather and my father when it came time to hand down the reigns to Maggie's Hideaway seemed to have been a smooth one, but I suspected the same was not true when it came time for Bradford to turn things over to Sterling.

Once Bradford had gone, I returned my attention to the tournament. By the time I finished my judging duties the sun had gone down. Kyle's game had finished before mine, so he'd gone to get us both burgers. He was on his way back in my direction just as I started toward the house. "Those look so good. I can't remember the last time I was this hungry."

"I got several different kinds. I figured we could cut them up and share."

Doc, Bookman, and Grandpa were all sitting on the front deck sharing a cold one when we arrived. Kyle and I sat down at the table on the front deck so we could brainstorm and eat at the same time. Normally, I would have joined the men in having a beer, but tonight I decided I was better off with coffee.

Kyle briefly caught everyone up with what had occurred and what we knew. Doc suggested that he call Roy or Kate to see if he could get more specific information relating to the findings in the autopsy. I just hoped Kate wouldn't be so pigheaded as to not allow Doc to consult. Kate had pointed out that Kyle and I were civilians on more than one occasion and should therefore stay out of her way, but Doc had been a professional and was better at what he had done than almost anyone.

"The part I'm having the hardest time with is the sequence of events," Bookman commented after Doc stepped inside to make his call. "Based on what you've described, Bristow was shot in the back, at which point it appears Gina, or whoever was driving her car, somehow got him into the vehicle; we assume to go for help. Why didn't she call 911 instead of moving him?"

"Kyle and I thought about that and felt the danger might still have been present," I responded. "Maybe whoever shot Bristow was a threat to her, so she couldn't afford to wait around."

"That works. For the sake of this conversation, let's just say the driver of the vehicle was Gina even though we don't know that for certain," Bookman said.

We all agreed.

"So Gina somehow managed to get the wounded Bristow into her car," Bookman continued. "It would make sense she'd head to the hospital. We don't know where the shooting occurred, so we can't know if the place where she ran off the road was between the location of the shooting and the hospital, but it's pretty far out of town."

"I've been thinking about that," Kyle said. "When Tj and I went to the crash site, we were followed. What if Gina was followed too and felt she needed to lose her tail, so she drove out of town."

Bookman sat forward and steepled his fingers. "It still makes sense she would have gone straight to the emergency room. It's unlikely she would have been accosted there because there are usually a lot of people around. However, if Gina had reason to think the shooter wanted her dead as well, I can see why she might have panicked and tried to lose him."

The thought that whoever had kidnapped Gina might want her dead sent chills down my spine. "Roy thinks if whoever attacked Gina wanted her dead, they would have killed her at the accident site."

"That's a good point," Bookman admitted. "Returning to the timeline, it appears something caused Gina to run off the road and hit the tree. It furthermore appears she was able to escape from the damaged car and head into the woods. We can assume she tried to hide, but whoever was after her followed and eventually caught up with her. It appears the assailant took her from the scene. My question is why?"

"Maybe the killer needs something from her," I suggested.

"That would explain how it could have gone down another way," Bookman said.

"Another way?" I asked.

"What if Bristow wasn't shot by someone with a grudge against him? What if he was shot by someone who was after Gina all along?"

The room fell into silence. Since the moment Kate had told me that Bristow had been found dead in Gina's car I had been operating under the assumption that it was Bristow the killer was after.

"Who would be after Gina?" I asked.

"I don't know, but it's an idea that makes sense," Bookman answered. He turned in his chair to more directly face me. "The kidnapper needs Gina for some reason. He tries to grab her, but Bristow intervenes, getting shot in the process. She manages to get the now-injured Bristow into the car and makes a run for it. She loses control of the car and ends up wrapped around a tree. She flees into the woods, but the person who tried to grab her in the first place is too quick and catches up with her."

I sat back in my chair. "So in this scenario, it's Bristow and not Gina who's the innocent bystander who gets caught in the crossfire."

"Basically."

"But which is it?" I asked. "How do we know if we're looking for someone in Gina's life or someone in Bristow's?"

"I don't suppose we can know. Not without additional information."

I glanced at Kyle, then back at Bookman. "A long-lost brother Gina doesn't know showed up in her life last week. As it turns out, a DNA test has proven he isn't related to her in any way. I've started to think his presence is linked to what happened in some way."

"Okay," Bookman said. "Let's take a few minutes to work up a suspect list where Gina is the intended victim. We should be looking at individuals who might need her for some reason rather than who might just want to kill her."

"Gina's a gifted mathematician," I began. "She has a doctorate in applied mathematics and worked in the private sector before coming to work at Serenity High School. I know very little about her past. It's possible there could be some big secret she's either protecting or trying to hide. And she took a leave last spring to work on some sort of secret project."

"Gina had a file stored in her Cybersecurity account that was protected with very sophisticated encryption," Kyle added. "I managed to get in, but the document I found is nothing more than a series of number sequences. I've got a program working on decoding it but haven't had any luck so far."

"So maybe Gina has some information someone wants," Bookman said. "Something top secret that would be valuable to a number of people."

"Poor Gina," I whispered. "I hope they aren't torturing her to try to get whatever it is they want from her."

Everyone was silent for a moment. The idea was beyond terrifying. While the conversation was on pause, Doc returned to the room, and we all looked at him.

"Were you able to speak to Kate?" I asked.

"I was," Doc confirmed. "She was actually very

cooperative."

"Well, at least we know she's willing to speak to someone other than Roy," I mumbled. "What did she say?"

"First, it appears Bristow bled out prior to the accident and therefore died from the gunshot wound before the vehicle hit the tree. The crime scene investigators believe Gina realized he was dead and tried to escape. Detective Baldwin still has no idea who was after her and no one has been able to pick up her trail after she left the woods for the road."

"If Gina was accosted by someone looking for intel on the project she worked on, they could be long gone by now," I said. "How will we ever find her?"

"What about the guy who isn't her brother?" Kyle asked. "Maybe we should take a closer look at him."

"Deputy Baldwin went by the house after receiving an anonymous 911 call regarding a prowler at the house on the night Gina went missing," Doc informed us. "The place was empty and the clothes you reported seeing in the guest room closet are no longer there. It's Deputy Baldwin's opinion the man has left the area."

"So what now?" I asked, a note of desperation clear in my voice.

"Let's start by taking another look around Gina's house," Doc suggested. "If the man was involved—and it appears he was—maybe he left something behind that will tell us where they've taken Gina."

"I still have the key," I volunteered.

"We'll all go," Bookman said. "We can take my van."

I wasn't holding out a lot of hope that we'd be able to find a clue that would lead us to Gina, but Doc had been good at what he did and Bookman had a mind for crime. Maybe if we all looked around together with the idea of finding physical evidence left behind, we could figure things out in time to save Gina. The more time that passed without us finding her the more likely it was that she would be dead when we finally did find her. For all I knew, she was dead now. I tried not to think about that. The last thing I needed was emotion clouding my judgement. Gina needed me to be strong for her.

Bookman parked in the driveway. We all piled out and entered the house through the front door. We decided Doc, Grandpa, and I would look around upstairs while Bookman and Kyle took a look downstairs.

The first thing I noticed was that there was something tracked all over the floor that hadn't been there when Kyle and I had been there on Thursday. At least, I didn't think it had. We had the overhead lights on now, and when Kyle and I were here before we'd only used flashlights, so it was possible we just hadn't noticed the brownish residue.

"What do you suppose this is?" I asked.

Grandpa bent over and took a closer look. "Appears to be sawdust."

"I agree," Doc said. "Maybe whoever took Gina has her stashed somewhere under construction."

I groaned. "It's summer in Paradise Lake. There's a lot of construction going on."

"Perhaps. It's still a clue," Doc said encouragingly. "You know, clues are like puzzle pieces that tell a story. Put enough together and a picture begins to emerge."

I looked around. "It's just that I'm beginning to feel desperate."

"That's completely understandable," Grandpa said before wrapping me in a tight hug.

Gina's bedroom didn't look like it had been touched since we'd been there last, but we knew Fake Spencer had been in the guest room to retrieve his clothes, so we focused our attention there. It would have been nice to find a piece of paper with an address or phone number, but all that was there was sawdust and red mud. There were a few places in the basin where one could find red dirt, but it wasn't at all common in town, so perhaps Gina was being held outside the developed area.

After we completed our search, we joined Kyle and Bookman downstairs. Bookman had found a leaf from a lilac bush. As far as I knew, Gina didn't have a lilac bush in her yard. The leaf was flattened, as if it had been tracked in on the bottom of a shoe. It hadn't rained in the past week but the mud we'd found upstairs and a leaf that had likely been stuck to a shoe seemed to indicate the ground had been wet.

"Okay, here's what we have," Doc began. "Sawdust, red mud, and a lilac leaf that appears to have been stuck to a shoe. What does that tell us?"

"New construction," Bookman put forth.

"It does seem that a building under construction that isn't currently being worked on would be a good place to stash someone," Grandpa said.

"There's that new warehouse out on the highway," Bookman said. "The owner had funding issues, and as far as I know, the contractor has stopped working on the building until the problem has been resolved."

"You would find sawdust there," Grandpa piped in.

"But not red mud or a lilac bush," I countered.

"A lot of people have lilac bushes in their yards," Kyle pointed out. "The moisture necessary for the leaf to stick to a shoe could have come from a lawn after watering."

"That's true," Doc said. "I'm not sure the leaf is an important clue."

"And there's a lot of construction going on, so the sawdust could have come from anywhere," Bookman added. "It seems the red mud might be the clue we should focus on."

"Wait," I said. "I remember seeing red mud on the floor of Gina's office on the night of the accident. I thought it looked as if it had been tracked in recently because the rest of the office was spotless. And when I left the office I heard footsteps. Damn. I bet Fake Spencer is behind this. I bet he was at the school and in Gina's house."

"There are several places you can find red dirt in this area," Grandpa told us. "Most are in higher elevations than the lake basin. If you combine the red mud with the sawdust, it seems we're looking for new construction up on the mountain."

"Maybe the Angel Mountain ski area. They've been undergoing a huge expansion over the past couple of years," Kyle said.

"Perhaps," Doc agreed. "But if Gina's being held at some new construction, it has to be a project not currently underway, or the workers would have seen her. I doubt the construction at Angel Mountain has gone dormant at this time in the year. The building season here is short. Unless there's a specific reason to halt construction, it would be worked on every day until it snows."

"What if the sawdust isn't from construction but maybe a lumber operation?" Bookman suggested.

"They're thinning the forest on the west shore," Ben provided.

"Lilac bushes don't grow wild, so it seems we're looking for a residence," Doc said.

"Unless the sawdust and lilac leaf were dragged in at different times," I said. "If we eliminate the lilac leaf and focus only on sawdust and red mud, there's going to be a lot of territory to search."

"It would seem we're looking for a building of some sort," Kyle pointed out.

"And a power source, if the men who kidnapped Gina are staying in the same area where they have her stashed," Doc added.

"Maybe they have her in one of the old forest service cabins up on the mountain," I suggested. "There's red clay where the cabins are located, and the cabins are powered by generators for the most part. I don't know about the sawdust, but I suppose the dust could even be a residue of chopping wood for a heat or cooking source."

Everyone paused to consider that possibility.

"Those old cabins seem to be as good a guess as any," Doc said at last. "There are quite a few, and they're spread out over a large area. The roads to them are primitive though, so it would take quite a while to check them all."

"We have to do something," I said.

"It's dark," Bookman said. "Unless we have a specific location to check, it would probably be best to wait for morning."

"Bookman is right," Doc seconded. "There doesn't seem to be much point in heading out now when lack of visibility is a factor."

"What about the static Kate heard from the handheld radio?" I asked. "Might it provide an additional clue?"

"How?" Grandpa asked.

"Roy told me the radio they found had a range of two or three miles. Kate picked up static from the device when she was driving on County Road 47, near the old dam. If we use that spot as ground zero, we should be able to figure out the general area where it originated."

Grandpa shrugged. "It's a long shot."

"True, but right now it's all we have. If we can narrow down the search area and then apply the sawdust and red mud filters, we might be able to narrow things down considerably."

"It's worth a try," Bookman agreed.

"Let's head back to the resort," Kyle suggested. "We'll need a map."

At the resort, Grandpa found a map of the area and laid it out on the dining table. Kyle put a red X on the spot where County Road 47 crossed the dam. Then he drew a giant circle with a three-mile radius.

"That's a lot of territory to cover," I said.

"Maybe, but the entire east side of the circle is lake level," Grandpa pointed out. "As far as I know, all the red dirt in the area is at around seven thousand feet."

Kyle drew lines through the part of the circle represented by an elevation below seven thousand feet.

"That helps, but it's still a lot," I said.

Grandpa pointed to the map. "This entire section over here is wilderness. If we assume whoever took Gina is holding her where there's shelter and a power source, we can eliminate this area as well."

Kyle drew lines through the area Grandpa indicated.

"It does seem this much smaller area should be our target." Bookman pointed to the smaller section that was left.

"There are cabins off the dirt road that used to service the old sawmill," Grandpa said. "If I were a betting man, I'd say we should start here. The cabins are rustic, powered by generators and wood burning stoves and heaters. None of them have plumbing. The cabins utilize outhouses and hand-dug wells. If I wanted to be close to town but still off the grid, this is where I'd hide out."

I looked at Kyle. "Let's check it out."

"We'll all go," Bookman said once again.

"Are you sure?" I asked. "It could be dangerous."

"Which is why we'll be safer in a group." Bookman looked at Grandpa. "You still have a couple of hunting rifles?"

"I do. Haven't used them in years, but I suppose they might still be functional."

Grandpa went for the rifles while Bookman used the gas pumps at the resort's filling station to top off his tank. Once we were ready, Kyle and I climbed into the van with our troupe of geriatric sleuths. I hated to put the men in danger, but I knew they were clearheaded adults able to make up their own minds.

There was only one road leading to the old forest service cabins. Bookman followed the highway until Grandpa told him to turn off onto a rutted dirt road. Even though Bookman had a four-wheel drive van, the going became rough. He drove, Grandpa sat in the passenger seat providing directions because he was the most familiar with the area, Doc sat in the middle seat chatting with them, and Kyle and I sat in the very back, holding hands and whispering to each other. It would have been sort of romantic if I wasn't so terrified. The closer we got to the old sawmill where most of the cabins were, the harder my heart seemed to pound.

"Once we reach the sawmill, there'll be two roads," Grandpa explained. "You'll see cabins dotted along both roads. The one to the right will take you farther up the mountain, while the one to the left runs parallel to the lake and mostly maintains a constant altitude. If I had to guess, our kidnappers would keep to the left."

"Especially if whoever was in the Ford Focus that followed us is part of this whole thing," I added. "The road that climbs the mountain demands four-wheel drive when you begin to climb. The one leading off to the left is accessible in most cars, although I imagine the undercarriage would get pretty torn up."

When we arrived at the sawmill, Bookman pulled over and turned off his headlights. "If we keep going in the van, they'll hear us coming," he pointed out. "I suggest a couple of us head out on foot and a couple stay back in case of emergency."

"I brought several of the radios we use at the resort so employees can communicate among themselves," Grandpa said. "They're short range, good for only a mile, but I wasn't sure what the cell reception would be up here."

"Kyle and I will go. The three of you wait here," I said. Grandpa was a spry old guy, but he'd already suffered one stroke. I didn't want him risking his health.

"I'll go with you," Bookman said. "Doc can stay with Ben."

Doc didn't argue, so I didn't either. Bookman was the youngest of the friends at fifty-nine, and he kept himself in pretty good shape.

Kyle, Bookman, and I took three of the radios and one of the rifles, while Grandpa and Doc held on to the fourth radio and the second rifle. The first of the cabins was only a hundred yards up the road or so, but from what I could tell, it was completely dark. I tried to breathe regularly as we approached, but no matter how hard I tried not to I couldn't help but hold my breath. After approaching the cabin, we walked toward the front of the structure and looked in the window. Although the interior was dark, from what we could see, the cabin was deserted.

"This could take all night," Kyle said.

"It could, but it seems to be our best bet," Bookman reminded him.

"Should we split up?' I asked.

Kyle shook his head. "Too dangerous."

We took our time, walking slowly and quietly and peeking into every cabin. We had no way to know if there was anyone inside, and whether they'd be asleep or awake if there was, but the lack of any sort of possessions or supplies as we looked through the windows seemed to indicate which were empty and which might have been recently occupied.

"Did you hear that?" I asked.

Everyone stopped walking.

"Hear what?" Kyle asked.

"A humming noise. It sounds like a swarm of bees."

Both Kyle and Bookman looked silently around the area. The sound was becoming fainter as we listened.

"I have no idea what that was, but I don't hear it any longer," Bookman whispered.

"Yeah, it's gone," I agreed.

"There are a lot of cabins in the area on generators. The noise we heard could have been a generator turning on and then off again," Kyle suggested.

I hoped he was right, because I couldn't get the idea of a lunatic with a chainsaw out of my mind.

Once we were convinced the sound we heard was gone, we continued on our way. The cabins in the area were more often vacant than occupied, but we did have the occasional visitor during the summer that was looking for a rustic experience.

"I see a light ahead," Kyle whispered.

We all stopped walking.

"Should we just go up and knock on the door?" I asked.

"It's a risk," Bookman answered.

"If we aren't going to check out occupied cabins, why are we even up here?" I demanded in a voice that sounded a lot angrier than I intended. "I'm sorry," I said in a softer tone of voice. "I guess the stress is getting to me."

"That's understandable," Bookman said, sympathy evident in his voice.

"How about if I go to the door alone. I'll pretend to be lost. If someone pulls me inside then the two of you can rally the troops and save me," I suggested.

"You're not going up to the house alone," Kyle insisted.

"It really is the best way." I glanced at Bookman. I could see that he agreed with me.

"It will be less suspicious if Tj goes alone," Bookman said.

"Unless the person who took Gina knows what she looks like," Kyle argued. "I'll go."

"But," I started.

Kyle didn't even respond. He just handed the gun to

Bookman and headed toward the door. I held my breath as Kyle knocked on the door and waited. A tall man with a plaid shirt answered. The men spoke for a minute and then Kyle went inside.

"What is he doing?" I screeched.

"Shhh," Bookman reminded me.

"We need to go and get him."

"Give him a minute."

I foolishly agreed to do so, not realizing it would be the longest minute of my life. Just when I had reached the point of going after Kyle in spite of Bookman's wishes, Kyle came back out. I let out the breath I'd been holding and waited.

"The men inside are here to fish. They all reported seeing a blue sedan coming and going on the road in front of the cabin, but they didn't know where the people in the blue sedan were staying."

"We were followed by men in a blue sedan," I said. "It could be them."

"I think we're in the right area," Kyle agreed.

"So what should we do now?" Bookman asked.

Kyle looked off into the distance. "Ben said the range on the walkies is a mile. Let's continue on to that point and then turn around if we haven't found anything."

Bookman and I both agreed.

It wasn't until we'd traveled almost to the end of that mile that I noticed a small cabin further off the road than the others. It was dark, but something about it caught my attention. After looking in the window as we'd been doing as we made our way up the road, I put a finger to my lips and tiptoed to the entry. I saw not only red mud on the stoop, but also a wild lilac bush near the front door.

"We need to look inside," I whispered.

Kyle and Doc nodded.

I slowly opened the door. Kyle went in first, carrying the rifle, I followed, and Bookman brought up the rear. The cabin appeared to be empty, but unlike the others, it had a lived-in feeling to it. Kyle crept to the bedroom door, holding the rifle in a ready-to-shoot position, while Bookman slowly opened the door. I glanced inside and gasped. "Gina."

CHAPTER 14

Sunday, August 13

When we found Gina last night, she was lying on the bed, passed out. At first, I thought she was dead, but then I realized she was breathing. We called for an ambulance and waited there for it to arrive. Once Gina was safely inside the emergency vehicle, we followed down the mountain. By the time we arrived at the hospital, Gina had been taken in for treatment. The woman at the ER reception desk didn't know anything, so we sat down to wait. It was after two a.m. by the time a doctor came out to tell us she was stable and resting comfortably. I wanted to see her, but he said she was asleep and wouldn't be able to talk to us until the following day. I didn't want to leave, but the others persuaded me to head home to get some shut-eye.

I must have fallen asleep in the van because the next thing I knew, I was waking up in my own bed. I looked over the side, expecting to see Echo, but he wasn't there. I didn't remember arriving at the resort, but it seemed Kyle carrying me to bed was quickly becoming our thing.

I rolled over and looked at the clock. It was eleven thirty.

Had I really slept that long? I certainly hadn't meant to, but it had been days since I'd had any decent sleep. Apparently, I'd been able to relax enough now that Gina was safe to allow my body to shut down and get the rest it needed.

After I made sure I was fully awake, I rolled out of bed and headed to the bathroom. I took a quick shower, then dressed in shorts and a tank top. I piled my wet hair on top of my head and went downstairs.

"There she is," Grandpa greeted me with a kiss on the cheek and a hot cup of coffee.

"I didn't mean to sleep so long. You should have woken me."

"No need," Grandpa said as he set a plate full of a stack of piping hot pancakes and crispy strips of bacon on the table. I sat down and opened the syrup. "Roy called and said he and Kate had spoken to Gina. He'll be by later to fill you in on the status of the investigation. In the meantime, he said Gina would be allowed visitors beginning at one."

"And Kyle?" I asked as I drizzled syrup over the pancakes.

"He went home after he got you tucked into bed. He said to call him when you got up and he'd come over with Echo."

I took a big bite of the sweet, fluffy pancakes. Suddenly, I was ravenous. When was the last time I'd even eaten? I guessed it must have been the two bites of hamburger I'd had the night before. "I'd like to go by to see Gina, but the girls will be home today."

"I can keep an eye on them if Jenna drops them off before you get back from the hospital."

"Thanks, Grandpa. I know you're busy, but I don't think I'll be able to relax completely until I see Gina awake with my own two eyes and hear her tell me she's okay."

"I understand. Now finish your pancakes. I'll call Kyle to tell him you're awake."

By the time I finished my second stack of pancakes and had washed them down with three cups of coffee, Kyle had arrived with Echo. After greeting them both, I went upstairs to finish getting ready. If Gina was allowed visitors at one o'clock, Kyle and I would be there at one o'clock on the dot.

"Last spring, I was working on a secret project for Jeremy Titan," Gina informed us after Kyle and I had confirmed she was indeed okay. She'd hit her head when her car hit the tree and had a mild concussion, so the doctor wanted to keep her overnight for observation. If all went well, she'd be released to go home the following day. In the meantime, Kyle and I were keeping her company. She'd already told Kate and Roy most of what she was telling us, but I found I preferred to hear it from her rather than secondhand from Roy. "Jeremy owns several large corporations, all operating under the umbrella of Titan Industries."

"I've heard of Titan and his companies," Kyle said. "He's a visionary who focuses on things that might move mankind forward in terms of technology, transportation, or communication."

"Exactly," Gina confirmed. I was happy to see her eyes were clear and her cheeks were pink. "The man's a total genius and he isn't afraid to chase an idea whether others think he has a chance of catching it or not. He's truly the most spectacular person I've ever met."

"So how did you manage to get hooked up with a guy like that?" I asked. "Not that you aren't brilliant and awesome in your own right," I quickly added.

Gina laughed. "I'm nowhere near Jeremy's league and I know it. I doubt I could even get near him now if I didn't already know him. Jeremy's an untouchable billionaire, but I was lucky enough to meet him a few years ago when I worked on a project of his while I was in grad school. It was a small project, mapping communication strings on the internet. Our findings didn't amount to a whole lot then, but in the short time we worked together, I realized he was not only brilliant, but also imaginative and hardworking. I was totally captivated. We became friends and, truth be told, I consider him one of my closest friends even today."

"Wow. I can't believe you're friends with Jeremy Titan," Kyle, who appeared to be starstruck, practically drooled. "Do you think you could introduce us?"

"Sure, if you're ever in DC."

"For the chance to meet Jeremy Titan, I'd make a special trip."

Gina smiled. "Okay, I'll set something up. Maybe you and Tj could take a romantic trip to the East Coast."

Kyle smiled and agreed a romantic trip sounded like just the thing, but to be honest, I wasn't sure I wanted to compete with someone like Jeremy Titan for Kyle's attention on the first couple's trip we took together. I didn't say as much, however. Instead, I asked, "So how does the fact that you participated in this project relate to what happened over the past couple of days?"

"The project I was recruited to work on this past spring was a new communications system called SCABS. I can't go into detail, but suffice it to say, the concept is unique and daring. All I did in April was work out the math needed to make the concept a reality based on the specs provided by a physicist, an engineer, and a few others who were also working on the project. Bringing the concept to reality won't be an inexpensive venture, but Jeremy has plans to build a prototype after he has the chance to sell the idea to a few investors."

That made sense. Even if you were a billionaire, it was smart to use other people's money when you could.

"Somehow, word about the project got out," Gina continued. "I don't know how the concept was leaked because very few people knew what we were doing, but someone must have talked. Anyway, I received a phone call from Jeremy at the end of June, saying he was going to have to move up the timeline he'd originally worked out to launch a working prototype so he could patent it before his competitor beat him to the starting gate. He wanted to know if I'd be available to meet with one of the astrophysicists working on the project, and I said I would. Jeremy said he'd be in touch with the details, so at that point I just went on with my life."

"What does this have to do with Bristow?" I asked.

"Hang on, I'm getting to that." Gina took a sip of water before she continued. "For you to understand everything, I'll need to weave several threads together chronologically, but in the end, you should have the whole picture."

"Okay. Sorry," I said. "Go on."

Gina nodded, then continued. "Right about the same time Jeremy contacted me, I found out my dad had had a heart attack. He and I aren't all that close and I hadn't seen him for quite some time, but my cousin called because he thought I should know what was going on, despite the fact that my dad had chosen not to call me to fill me in himself. According to my cousin, Dad was fine and even home already, but he said his insurance had lapsed and it looked as if he was going to lose his home if he couldn't come up with the money to pay the hospital at least part of what he owed. I wanted to help, but I didn't have nearly enough saved, so I put out a few feelers to friends and associates, letting them know I was looking for some summer work. A few days later, I was contacted by Striker Bristow. He had a development he was trying to get approved and he thought he might need help to do it. I'm not sure where he got my name, but he was offering me an obscene amount of money for only a couple of months' work. I decided to meet with him and look at his proposal. It wasn't bad, but it did need some work, so I decided to take him up on his offer. I knew I could help him develop a plan that would meet his goals and benefit the community, and in the process, I would earn the money I needed to help my dad with his debt."

I wanted to point out that Bristow was an ass and therefore unworthy of Gina's help, but I decided to hold my tongue, especially because the reason she needed the money was a good one.

"About a week after I signed on with Striker," Gina went on, "I received an email from a man claiming to be my half-brother. I hadn't seen Spencer since I was a toddler and didn't remember him at all. We shared a mother who died when I was just two, but because we were both raised by our fathers, we hadn't crossed paths. I thought the timing a little odd, but I'd always wanted to meet him, and he seemed to know things only my brother would know. I agreed to have him come here for a visit, but almost immediately after he arrived and we spent time together, I started to have my doubts about him."

"Which is why you asked Hunter to do a DNA test," I supplied.

"Exactly."

I waited while Gina took another sip of water.

"Meanwhile," Gina continued, "the work with Striker was moving right along. I was happy with what we'd come up with, as was he. All we really needed to do was sell it to the town council, so Striker gave me an advance on the money he'd promised me so I could make a payment toward my dad's debt. I didn't want him to know what I was doing, so I asked the hospital to tell him they'd made an adjustment and were going to take another look at the total and get back to him. That bought me time to finish the project with Striker and get the rest of the money he owed me."

"You must have felt the project would be approved," I said.

"I hoped it would. I knew there was some opposition, but I thought the overall plan really worked. Striker and I had been meeting with town council members, and I felt like he had the support he needed."

"So how does this all relate to Bristow being shot and you being imprisoned in a forest service cabin?" I asked, bringing the conversation back around to what I was most interested in.

"I'm getting to that," Gina said. "Remember, I told you there were several things that were all going on simultaneously."

"You did. I forgot. Go on."

"About a week ago, I was contacted by a man who claimed to work for Jeremy's biggest competitor. He offered me a lot of money to share with him the specifics of the project I'd been working on. I turned him down, of course, and called Jeremy, who told me other members of the team had been contacted as well. He was more than a little angry but not overly concerned because he felt we had enough of a head start to get our prototype off the ground first, even if the competition was successful in gaining the information they needed. I decided I didn't need to worry about it if he wasn't overly concerned. That was when he asked me to move up the timeline to meet with the astrophysicist he'd been telling me about. His name was Carter Kline, and we agreed to meet at Murphy's on Wednesday."

"Why Murphy's?" I asked, interrupting again. "Wouldn't your house have been a better place?"

"It would seem, but Jeremy didn't want anyone to realize Kline and I had met. Spencer was staying with me by then, so I thought Murphy's would be a low-profile place to meet. I didn't know Kline would show up in a full suit in the middle of summer. He really stuck out like a sore thumb."

"Yeah, he did," I said. "Several people mentioned it."

"In retrospect, Murphy's wasn't the best choice, but by the time I realized it, it was too late."

"Then what happened?" I asked, anxious to hear more.

"Thursday was a busy day. I'd promised to volunteer at the wakeboard competition in the morning and I had a lunch date with Striker. In addition to that, I'd offered to go out to the land where the mall was to be built to take some photos and measurements. And I had a sick friend I wanted to check in on and a dinner date with one of the town councilmen. In the midst of what turned out to be a lot of running around, I spotted a blue sedan following me pretty much everywhere I went."

"The blue car followed us as well," I replied. "After we'd been to your house, trying to find you."

"It turns out the blue sedan was Spencer, or the man pretending to be Spencer, and his partner Arnie, although I didn't realize that at the time."

"Did you notify the sheriff?" Kyle asked.

"No. I mean, no one had done anything illegal. I just had a funny feeling about things, so I didn't have anything to report. Anyway, back to Thursday of last week." Gina took a deep breath. "As I mentioned, Striker had asked me if I would attend a meeting he'd set up with council member Doug Conrad. They planned to meet at the Lakeview Restaurant and I was to meet them there after the bake-off, where I was going to buy a cake for my friend. Conrad loved our ideas, and everything was going well until we were ready to leave the marina. Striker and I walked Doug out to his car and he left. Striker walked me to my car and I'd just unlocked the driver's side door and was preparing to get in when I noticed blood on his shirt."

"You didn't hear a gunshot?" Kyle asked.

"No, I didn't hear a thing. The gun must have had a silencer. I had no idea anything was going on until I saw the blood. Striker didn't even call out. I think he was stunned."

"What did you do?" I asked.

"I ran around to the passenger side of my car and shoved him into the passenger seat, then I ran back around to the driver's side, started the car, and took off. I didn't hear anything or see anyone with a gun, so I thought we'd gotten away. I was planning to drive to the hospital, but I noticed the same dark blue sedan behind us. I sped up and it did too. Looking back on things, I should have gone straight to the hospital, but I panicked. Instead of going there, I made a hard right turn onto the highway, trying to lose our tail."

"You must have been so scared," I sympathized.

"I was. I was convinced whoever was in the blue sedan had shot Striker and they were coming after us to shoot me too. As you already know, things went from bad to worse when I made the decision to try to outrun my tail. I ended up overcorrecting on a sharp curve and ran off the road, hitting a tree. I was pretty sure Striker was already dead. He'd lost a lot of blood and had passed out shortly after we left the marina. Now he was completely unresponsive. I didn't have time to try to help him, I just ran. I thought I might get away, but one of the men—the passenger, who I later found out was Arnie—had gotten out of the car and followed me. He managed to catch up to me just before I got to the road on the other side of the forest. His buddy, the man I thought was my brother, was waiting with the car. They forced me in and took me to the cabin near the old sawmill."

"Why did they take you?"

"They wanted the mathematical formula for the communication system I'd worked out for Jeremy. They were convinced I had all the pieces, which I didn't.

"But why had they been following you around? And why go to all the trouble to place a fake brother in your house? Why not just grab you in the first place?"

"They knew I was meeting with Kline, but they didn't know what he looked like or where we'd meet. They'd also picked up a false rumor that Jeremy Titan himself would be in town. Jeremy is well protected and virtually untouchable in DC. I think they'd decided to bide their time and follow me around in the hope of bagging not just me, but perhaps Carter and Jeremy as well."

"I guess that makes sense. What happened next?" I asked. "Except for you, the cabin was empty when we found you, so where are they now?"

"Gone. They received a call at some point on Friday evening and took off. They left me tied to the bed with a head injury and absolutely no food or water. I would have died if you hadn't found me."

I took Gina's hand in mine. "I'm so sorry you had to go through all that. You must have been terrified."

"I was, but somewhere deep inside I knew you'd be looking for me. More than anyone I know, you always make sure the people you care for are all right."

Gina's words touched my heart. I squeezed her hand. "So I guess the only unanswered question is, why did they shoot Bristow?"

"That's the odd part. They didn't. While they held me, I overheard them talking. When Striker was shot, they were just following me, hoping I'd lead them to Kline. They were as shocked as anyone when they realized Striker had been shot. Of course, once I took off, they continued to follow me, as they had been all day. Although they might very well be responsible for Striker's death, because I would have gone straight to the hospital instead of trying to run if they hadn't been following me, I'm convinced they weren't responsible for him being shot in the first place."

"So if the men who detained you didn't shoot Bristow, who did?"

"I have no idea."

CHAPTER 15

Thursday, August 17

It had been several days since we'd rescued Gina and life seemed to have returned to normal. Kyle and I never did have our romantic evening together, which was playing heavy on my mind, but my sisters were home and I had responsibilities to attend to. When we finally did take the next step in our relationship, I wanted it to be perfect, not rushed.

Jeremy Titan had notified the FBI of his situation, and the men responsible for kidnapping Gina had been arrested in Maryland. As we suspected, it appeared that the brains behind the entire operation was Jeremy's main competitor, Huntington Enterprises. The problem was that Huntington had covered his tracks, and in the end, he got off scot free while one of his thugs was framed for the whole thing.

We still had no idea who'd shot Bristow and, to be honest, for a while I didn't care. The only reason I'd become involved was because Gina had been in trouble, but once she was safe, my interest in the whole thing pretty much faded.

At first.

And then I ran into Kate at the Antiquery.

"No need to thank me for finding Gina," I said in a sarcastic tone of voice that was mean even for me. I hated the fact that Kate seemed to bring out the worst in me, but as hard as I tried, which really wasn't all that hard, I just couldn't seem to avoid goading her.

"I understand that you had help from Stan Griffin, who, as I will remind you, was a professional trained in matters relating to murder investigations."

"That is true," I admitted. Doc, a.k.a Stan Griffin, had helped out, as had Bookman, Grandpa, and Kyle.

"I am happy that Ms. Roberts was found safe, but I want you to understand without a shadow of a doubt that your success in this one isolated incidence should in no way be perceived as permission to butt your nose in where it doesn't belong. I have said this before and I will say it again. If you want to run around doing the work of a law enforcement officer, go to the academy and get the training you need. One of these days your tendency to play cop is going to get you killed, and the last thing I need is your death on my conscious."

With that she walked out.

"Well, I never," I said to Jenna who was standing nearby.

"Don't let her get to you. Gina is safe and the case is closed. Would you like some pie?"

"No. Thanks for lunch, but I should be going. Is Dennis off this weekend?"

"The entire three days," Jenna grinned.

"Let's the four of us go out. It's been forever. I'll call you tomorrow."

After I left the Antiquery I tried to put my altercation with Kate out of my mind, but that seemed like an impossible task. Gina was safe, but Kate and Roy still hadn't managed to bring Bristow's killer to justice and I felt the old itch begin to scratch at my consciousness just a bit. I hadn't meant to become involved in this murder, but almost against my own will, I found myself reviewing the facts Kyle and I had gathered over and over in my mind. I know I'm not a cop and it isn't my responsibility to solve every murder occurring in Serenity, but I'm a competitive sort and the more someone—namely Kate—tells me not to do something, the more I want to do it.

We now had a timeline and we knew a lot about what had happened. Gina had volunteered at the wakeboarding completion on the morning Bristow had died. They'd had lunch that afternoon before each had gone their separate ways. Gina had told me that after lunch she'd driven out to the proposed mall site and taken some photos while Bristow caught up on some paperwork in his office. While at the mall site, Gina had walked and made a few notes. According to what we'd been told by Connie Bristow, she'd been at his office trying to collect the money he owed her, while Gina was at the bake-off buying a cake for her friend. After Bristow's ex-wife left his office he'd gone over to the marina restaurant to meet Doug Conrad to try to ensure his vote for the mall project. After Gina dropped off the cake, she'd driven over to the restaurant to join them.

When the meeting with the town council member was over, Gina and Bristow had walked Conrad to his car, and then Bristow walked with Gina to her car, where he was shot. According to Gina, the fact that Bristow had been shot had nothing to do with the men who were following and eventually kidnapped her. But the fact that those two unrelated things were going on at the same time seemed unimaginable. And while I'd never been a fan of the dishonest businessman, the events surrounding his death had worked their way under my skin. I wasn't sure I could let them go.

I hadn't mentioned to anyone, including Kyle, that I'd been making a few notes. Now I felt perhaps the time had come to bring him into the loop.

First, though, I needed to have breakfast with my family and make sure the chores at the resort were covered and the girls were taken care of for the day.

"Good morning, everyone," I greeted as I joined my dad and his fiancée Rosalie, Grandpa, and Ashley and Gracie at the breakfast table. Grandpa had made scrambled eggs and sausage with home-baked bread. I was starving. "What does everyone have going on today?"

"Kristi wants to come over," Ashley informed me. "We're going to go swimming and then maybe hang out on the beach."

"Sounds fun," I replied. "Remember, it's fine to swim in the pool, but no swimming in the lake without an adult to supervise."

"I'm going to be in middle school this year," Ashley complained. "I'm old enough to swim in the lake without a babysitter."

Ashley did have a point. She was a good swimmer, as was Kristi, and I'd been allowed to swim in the lake unsupervised when I was in middle school. I glanced at my dad, who looked away. I knew he wanted me to make my own decisions when it came to the girls. I didn't blame him for not wanting to get into the middle of things. "How about we talk to Jenna to see how she feels about it?"

Ashley shrugged. "Okay, but she'll be fine with it. Kristi and I went swimming in the lake by ourselves when we were camping."

"They did," Gracie said in support of her older sister.

"If Jenna was okay with you and Kristi swimming in the lake, I guess we can try it. But I want you to stay on the beach to the right of the marina where there are a lot of people around, just in case."

"Just in case of what?" Ashley asked.

"I don't know. *Just in case* is a blanket statement adult use. Do we agree?"

"Sure. That's the best beach anyway."

I turned my attention to my younger sister. "How about you? Do you have plans for the day?"

"Me and Kari are going to the new Disney movie with her grandma if it's okay with you."

"It's fine with me. I'll talk to Jenna about it when I call her." I looked at my dad. "Are you planning to work in the lodge today?"

"I am." Dad still couldn't get around the way he had before his accident, but he wanted to get back into a normal routine, so he'd set up an office in the lodge where he could sit for most of the day and still be in the center of things. "Rosalie will be busy with the spay-and-neuter clinic today, so I thought I'd have lunch with Noah. We can discuss plans for the ski season."

"Ski season? It's still August," Ashley said.

"The snow will be here before you know it," Dad informed her, though she didn't look at all thrilled with the idea.

"You might want to begin making plans for Winter Carnival," I suggested. "Sterling Snow has been chomping at the bit to begin."

"I've spoken to him and am in the process of gathering the information he's looking for," Dad told me.

"I don't know why he's so worked up, though I suppose Winter Carnival is his biggest moneymaker and Kyle mentioned the town council is looking to up the ante and do something really spectacular this year."

"It seems like it's already pretty special," Grandpa said.

"Yeah, I like ice skating and the snowman contest," Gracie added.

"And the pageant for winter princess," Ashley piped in.

"I agree that what we already have is awesome, but I guess Mammoth realized what a great moneymaker we have with Winter Carnival and is doing their own event this year. Kyle and the rest of the town council just want to make sure we stay ahead of the competition."

"I've always thought the ice fishing derby should be longer than just one day," Grandpa voiced his opinion.

"If anyone has suggestions, now's the time to make them," Dad said.

"I think school should be canceled for the whole week," Ashley said.

"I don't think that's something the Winter Carnival committee has control over," I pointed out as I poured myself another cup of coffee.

I really loved these family meals and would miss them if the girls and I moved out someday.

"What are you doing today?" Gracie asked me after I sat

back down at the table.

"I'm meeting Gina for lunch and then I thought I'd go visit with Uncle Kyle for a while. It's been so busy this week, we've barely had a minute to catch up."

"You just want to play kissy-face." Gracie giggled.

"I guess I can't pull anything over on you," I admitted.

"How's Gina doing?" Rosalie asked.

I lifted one shoulder. "Okay, I guess. Physically, I think she is, but I have a feeling she's struggling emotionally. Her ordeal must have been very traumatic. One of the reasons I invited her to lunch today was to check in with her, see how she's doing."

"She might want to talk to someone," Grandpa said. "Perhaps a counselor. Being held captive and having your free will stripped from you can be terrifying. It can leave you feeling raw and vulnerable."

I stabbed the last piece of sausage and popped it into my mouth. "I spoke to Sheila about that. She has a friend who's a psychotherapist. She tried to talk to her about seeing her, but Gina insisted she was totally fine. Gina's always been a strong person, but now that some time has passed, I wouldn't be a bit surprised to find things are beginning to hit her. I guess all I can do is be a friend."

"Speaking of friends, Doc and Bookman are picking me up in an hour," Grandpa said as he began clearing dishes.

"Are you going sailing?" I asked.

"Yes. Bookman's thinking about getting a new boat and he managed to arrange for a demo later this morning."

"Didn't Bookman get a new boat a couple of years ago?" I asked.

"He did, but this would be a new, new boat. We have to

drive down to Indulgence for the demo, so we're having lunch at that new restaurant in the village."

"Sounds like fun. Go ahead and get ready. I'll take care of the dishes," I offered.

By the time I'd cleaned up, it was almost time for Helen to come by with Kristi. The plan was for her to drop Kristi off to spend the day with Ashley and pick Gracie up to spend the day with Kari. I was forever grateful to both Jenna and her mother for making sure my girls were entertained. I didn't know what I'd do without them. Of course, Helen might not be quite as available once she and Bookman were married. They'd decided to have the wedding in November when the resort was closed during the off-season lull. I was excited they wanted to get married at the resort, but worried that hosting such a big event would be hard on Dad. The staff, after all, would be off for their own pre-ski season holiday. But November was three months away, and his recovery had been progressing a lot faster than any of us could have hoped. Besides, Jenna would be in charge of the wedding planning, and if there was anyone who could do the impossible, it was my best friend.

"Wow! It's really a beautiful day," Gina said as we had lunch at the Lakeside Bar and Grill. I'd reserved the best table on the patio, tucked into a secluded corner with sand on two sides and the lake on the third. "You're really very lucky to live here. It must be so nice to be able to enjoy the peace and tranquility of the lake every day."

"It is pretty amazing," I had to admit. "You're more than welcome to come here and hang out with me anytime you feel the need for a little peace and tranquility of your own."

"Actually, I wanted to talk to you about that." Gina took a sip of her iced tea. It appeared as if she was working up to sharing something big. "I want to start by saying how very much I appreciate all you did to find and rescue me. I owe you my life."

"Nonsense. You're my friend. Of course I was going to look for you. Kyle too. And I know you would have done the same if it had been me who was missing."

"Perhaps. But you have a unique ability not only to care deeply about the well-being of others, but also to put action to your caring. Not everyone would put themselves on the line the way you do time and time again. You're truly a unique and wonderful person."

"Aw, Gina." I leaned forward and hugged her. "Thank you. You're pretty awesome yourself."

Gina smiled but didn't respond. She looked tired. It must be hard to sleep after going through what she had.

"Are you doing okay?" I asked.

Gina sighed. "I've been better. I've given things a lot of thought in the past few days and I've decided to take a leave of absence from the school."

I was surprised to hear that. Gina loved teaching.

"I spoke to Jeremy and he's offered me a job," Gina continued. "He wants me to help him with the prototype now that he's definitely decided to go ahead with his plans. At first I wasn't sure I wanted to move to DC, but after everything that's gone on in the past week, I realized a change of scenery is exactly what I need."

I frowned. "Are you leaving for good?"

Gina tilted her head to one side. The sun reflected off her glasses as she angled her head toward the sun. "I don't know. Maybe. I'm going to keep my house for now and see how it goes in DC. If things work out the way I hope, I may decide to make the move permanent. I guess I'll just need to take things one day at a time."

I sat back in my chair, studying Gina's face. "I'm going to ask you a question I know is really none of my business. You don't have to answer if you don't want to."

"Okay."

"I know that prior to coming to Paradise Lake you worked in the private sector. Something must have happened to make you leave that behind to take a job in our little high school. Did that have anything to do with Jeremy Titan?"

Gina hesitated, but I could see she was deciding what to say. Eventually, she began to speak. "Prior to coming to Serenity High School, I not only worked with Jeremy, we were involved. I loved him with all my heart, but at the time it seemed the only thing he could ever truly love was his work. I wanted more, so I left. That was three years ago. Then, last spring, he asked me to help with his new project. I almost turned him down, but the concept intrigued me. I figured that although it was Jeremy's company behind the project, he was a busy man and I probably wouldn't even see him. I was wrong. I saw him quite a lot. We kept our relationship professional, but I felt the old magic again and I suspected he did as well. After the first phase of the project was complete, he wanted me to stay, but I turned him down. I didn't want to make the same mistake with him a second time."

"And now?" I asked when Gina paused.

"When the men who kidnapped me gave up and left me

alone to die, I was terrified. Looking death in the face can make you look back on your life. Somehow, the prospect of death demands that you look objectively at the decisions you've made, the good and the bad. I realized my biggest mistake was leaving Jeremy rather than sticking around and trying to work it out. I knew at that moment that I wanted a second chance. Jeremy flew out here this past Monday and we spent a few days together. He told me that he wanted a second chance too. We decided we'd take some time to get reacquainted, so I'm just going to DC as an employee, at least in the beginning. It will give us a chance to explore whatever it is that may be between us out of the public eye."

"Wow." I put a hand to my heart. "That's so romantic."

Gina laughed. "Maybe, but the truth of the matter is, I'm terrified. I don't think I can stand it if things don't work out and I'm forced to leave Jeremy behind again."

I took Gina's hand in mine. "It'll work out. You're a different person than you were three years ago. You know what you want. And although I've never met Jeremy, he sounds like a smart guy. I'm sure he's learned some lessons along the way as well."

Gina wiped a tear from her cheek. "I hope so."

I sat back and smiled. "Kyle's going to be so jealous that you're moving to DC to work with his hero," I joked to lighten the mood.

"Speaking of Kyle, I spoke to Jeremy about him and he wants to meet him. He didn't want anyone to know he was here earlier in the week, but he wants me to arrange a dinner meeting with Kyle once I get settled in DC. I'd love it if you could come as well."

"I'd love that, and Kyle will be over the moon."

"He did seem pretty starstruck. Jeremy might be brilliant and rich, but he's just a regular guy. I think Kyle and Jeremy are going to be great friends, which works out for you and me because that means we can continue to see each other."

"That sounds perfect."

Gina and I didn't speak as our food was delivered. I wanted to ask her some questions I had regarding Bristow's murder, but I hated to bring him into what had turned out to be a perfectly lovely conversation. As it turned out, it was Gina who mentioned him later, as we waited for our dessert.

"While I'm excited to start a new chapter of my life, I do find Striker Bristow is on my mind," Gina said. "I can't help but feel partially responsible for his death. Not that it was my fault he was shot—I think he may have brought that on himself—but if the men who were following me hadn't been following us, I'm fairly certain I would have gotten him to the hospital in time to save his life."

"As much as I didn't care for him, I've been thinking about Bristow's death as well," I said. "I hoped Roy and Kate would have made an arrest by now, but it appears they're stumped. I hate to remind you of something so traumatic, but do you have any idea who might have shot him?"

Gina crossed her arms on the table in front of her and looked out to the lake.

I went on softly. "Before we realized your kidnapping was most likely not related to Bristow's project, Kyle and I came up with four names: Byron Wildman, the man who lives behind the lot where Bristow wanted to build the mall; Clint Buford, who was suing Bristow for an unpaid invoice; Billy Sparks, who was very much against the project and meant to fight it on behalf of the environmental group to which he belonged; and Connie Bristow, his ex-wife. We pretty much eliminated Sparks and Mrs. Bristow. We spoke to Wildman, but never came to a conclusion about him."

Gina leaned slightly forward. "I agree Billy Sparks didn't shoot Striker. We spoke several times and my impression was that he knew how to fight the environmental battle using the legal system. The group he's a part of has deep pockets, and even if they don't win the battle, they'd be able to keep the project tied up in court for so long, most developers would give up. Striker was as stubborn as they come and swore he'd fight to the end for his right to do what he wanted with the property, but I'm not so sure he wouldn't eventually have given up."

"And the others?" I asked.

"I never met Mrs. Bristow, but from things he said, I had the impression he enjoyed feuding with her. I know that sounds strange, but it seemed to me he intentionally yanked her strings because he liked the banter. Now, I have no way of knowing whether she enjoyed playing his little game as much as he enjoyed manipulating her."

"I got the impression she wasn't his biggest fan. She said he made her grovel for the monthly support checks he owed her rather than just giving them to her."

"I suppose if I had an ex who made me jump through a bunch of hoops like a trained dog, I might shoot him," Gina said.

"It would be tempting. I couldn't imagine why she would have kidnapped you after shooting Bristow, so Kyle and I pretty much discounted her, but now that I know the two things weren't related, I think we'll have to put her back on the list."

"You have a list?" Gina asked.

"We did. I'm not sure what happened to it, but it seems it might be time for a new one. What do you think about Wildman as a suspect?"

"Personally, I like him for the murder. He's been very vocal about his hatred for Striker from the beginning, and unlike Billy Sparks, who had a strong nonviolent way to fight him, I don't think Wildman had a legal option."

"Yeah, he did seem sort of rough and tumble. Like the kind of guy who settles things with his fists, rather than in court," I said.

"I saw Wildman on the day Striker was shot," Gina informed me. "Remember, I told you that I'd gone out to the property where Striker hoped to build the mall? While I was taking photos and measurements, Wildman was standing on his side of the fence watching me. He never said a word, but his presence gave me the creeps. I couldn't wait to get out of there."

"How would he know Bristow was going to be at the restaurant?" I asked.

"I don't know. And maybe he wasn't the shooter. But I wouldn't take him off the list just yet."

"The only reason we didn't consider him a more serious suspect was because he didn't seem to know Bristow was dead. I suppose he could just be a good actor." I motioned for our waitress, then asked her to bring me a pen and a piece of paper. As long as we were making a theoretical list, we may as well make a real one. "And Clint Buford?" I asked.

Gina tapped her fingers on the table. She twisted her lips in thought before answering. "Buford was as mad at Striker as I've ever seen a man, but I'm not sure what he had to gain by shooting him. Striker owed him money and he was being a jerk about paying him, but if Buford pursued the matter legally, it seemed to me he would have won. I think Striker would have gone ahead and paid him before it got that far. He liked to play with people, but he wasn't stupid. I doubt he would have thrown good money after bad by paying to defend a lawsuit he knew he'd probably lose. Wouldn't Buford be less likely to get his money if Striker was dead?"

"Kyle said something similar. I guess that's why we didn't pursue him as a suspect." I glanced down at my piece of paper. "So, I have Wildman and Mrs. Bristow. Does anyone else come to mind?"

"I know Striker had a lot of enemies. There's one person who stands out in my mind: Glen Yorkshire. He tracked me down last week because he was sure his wife, Isabelle, was having an affair with Striker. He'd asked both of them about it, and they denied it, but he wasn't pacified. He hoped I'd seen them together, that I had something to give him that would prove they were seeing each other."

Glen worked for the IT firm the school used to maintain its computer system, so I had met him on several occasions. He was an intelligent if not slightly awkward man who I knew had been married for a number of years. I supposed it was possible his wife had tired of her husband who seemed to work a lot of hours.

"Do you think they were?"

Gina shrugged. "I have no idea. I know Striker had women, but I tried very hard to stay out of that part of his life. I told Yorkshire as much, but I'm not sure he believed me. I only spoke to him the one time and can't claim to know if he's capable of murder, but he was smoking hot when we spoke, so I wouldn't be all that surprised to find out he did it."

I added Glen Yorkshire to the list. "Anyone else?"

"No one else comes to mind right now. I'll call you if I think of anyone else."

I set the piece of paper aside. "When are you going to leave town?"

"I have a flight on Saturday, but I'll be back. If it works out and I do decide to stay in DC, I'll need to have my stuff sent out there."

"I'm really going to miss you."

Gina leaned forward and hugged me. "I'm going to miss you too. But we'll see each other."

I nodded. "We will. Kyle will definitely want to come to DC to meet Jeremy, and now that I know you'll be there, I'll be excited to come as well."

"If you think of anything relating to Striker's murder you want to ask about, feel free to call me. I'll feel better when this whole thing is wrapped up and put to bed."

"Actually, I have two more questions before you go."

"Okay."

"We found a phone in the water near Rosenberg Island that looked like it might have been yours, but it sounds like you were never there."

"I wasn't. I don't know what happened to my phone; I dropped it somewhere along the way. Someone may have found it, or it could be that the phone you found wasn't mine. I have a pretty popular cover."

"I should ask Roy. He's probably figured out whether the phone was yours or not. After we found you it didn't seem to matter anymore, so I never did ask. It didn't work anymore, so I don't suppose you'd want it back."

"I don't," Gina confirmed. "You said you had two questions?"

"The file Kyle found in your online storage. The one with the extra security. Does it relate to the project you were working on?"

"It does. Let me guess: Kyle is trying to figure out what the number sequences mean."

"He was before we found you, but I don't know if he continued after you were found. I was just curious."

"You can tell Kyle the numbers are one piece of a whole that mean nothing in isolation, so he may as well save his time. There isn't anything there to decrypt."

"I will. He probably isn't working on it anyway, but it crossed my mind. I guess you got everything back we took while trying to find you? We turned it all over to Kate at her insistence."

"I got everything back that matters, although I'm missing some birth control pills."

I blushed. "Oops. I forgot about those. I stuck them in my bag along with some cream prescribed to Spencer Becker. How did the fake Spencer get hold of the real Spencer's cream?"

"I'm not sure. It looks like Fake Spencer was in Paradise Lake on behalf of Colton Huntington. Huntington is both rich and well-connected. I guess he must have found out about Real Spencer somehow and tracked him down. I have no idea how he got his hands on the cream. It might have even been a fake prescription provided to Fake Spencer to convince me that the man who showed up at my door actually was my brother. I guess it worked. At first. I really am not privy to all the details relating to everything that went down last week, nor do I even care at this point. I really just want to forget about the whole thing."

"Trust me, I don't blame you a bit for wanting to just let the Feds figure it out."

"One good thing has come out of this mess however. I realized that I did want to get to know my half-brother. I tracked him down and found out he lives in Maryland. We're going to get together when I get settled in DC."

I squeezed Gina's hand. "I'm so glad. Family is the most important thing there is."

CHAPTER 16

Later that afternoon, Echo, Pumpkin, and I headed over to Kyle's. Pumpkin was actually Gracie's dog, but she wasn't at home and I knew he'd enjoy taking a walk with Kyle, Trooper, Echo, and me. I was sad that Gina was leaving Paradise Lake, but after thinking things through I realized that making this move was probably for the best. I hoped things worked out with both Jeremy and her brother. Gina was such a great person, she deserved to be happy.

"I have news," I said to Kyle after Echo, Pumpkin, and I had greeted Trooper, who had run out onto the drive.

"What kind of news?" Kyle asked after delivering a quick peck on my lips.

"Gina is moving to DC to work with Jeremy Titan. As it turns out, before moving to Paradise Lake, Gina was involved in a romantic relationship with him. Apparently, he wants them to try to work things out."

"Lucky Gina. It would be so awesome to work with that man." Kyle kissed me again before taking my hand and leading me toward the house. "Of course, there's no one I'd rather work with than you."

I laughed. "Nice save, but I'm fine with your bromance with

Jeremy Titan. Based on what Gina has told me, he seems like an awesome guy. Gina has invited both of us to DC once she gets settled. She told Jeremy about you and he very much wants to meet you."

"Jeremy Titan wants to meet me?"

"Yup."

I could see he was trying not to make too big a deal about it. Kyle was usually so methodical and mature. It was fun to see him on the edge of giving in to the urge to jump up and down with excitement.

"And Gina told me the numbers you uncovered were part of a whole that mean nothing in isolation, just in case you're still working on them."

Kyle shook his head. "I stopped working on the file the minute Gina was found. Whatever she had saved in her Cybersecurity account is none of my business, and the only reason I invaded her privacy was to try to find her. Did Roy return her computer to her?"

"She said she got everything back except her birth control pills, which I forgot I had in my bag. She has since refilled the prescription, so I guess I'll just dispose of them."

"The dogs seem pretty wound up," Kyle commented as we watched them wrestling around with each other.

"Let's take them for a walk," I suggested. "We can talk and walk at the same time."

I wanted to fill Kyle in on my plan to begin looking into Bristow's case once again and figured this would be as good a time as any. Kyle didn't seem as certain about getting involved in things as I'd remained, but as I shared the specifics Gina and I had discussed over lunch, I could see him become more invested in the idea.

"You know," Kyle said after throwing a stick into the lake, which all the dogs took off after, "a big part of the problem when we started our list was that we couldn't imagine who would both shoot Bristow and kidnap Gina. Now that we know the two things aren't necessarily related, several other people come to mind."

"It just occurred to me that the men who were following Gina might know who shot Bristow. If they were waiting for Gina to come out of the restaurant, they must have been parked nearby."

"Good point. I wonder if they'd be willing to tell us what they know," Kyle said.

"I know they're in FBI custody. I guess it wouldn't hurt to call Roy and have him see what he can find out. In the meantime, we can come up with a list of people to talk to. It seems like we've had as much luck tracking down killers in the past as anyone."

"Along the same line of thought as Gina's kidnappers perhaps having seen the shooting, it's entirely possible anyone who was in the marina's parking lot might have seen something as well," Kyle said.

"That's true. But don't you think a casual observer might have called the sheriff's office?"

"Not necessarily. A lot of people don't want to get involved. A lot of the marina customers are tourists who would be gone by now, but there are resident slips, so if we ask around, we might find someone who was there on the evening Bristow was shot."

"Doug Conrad," I said. "Gina told me that she and Bristow first walked Doug to his car, and then Bristow walked Gina to hers. Doug could have seen something when he was leaving, and even if he was gone by the time the shot was fired, he might have noticed someone suspicious lurking around as he pulled out."

"We should talk to Doug. I'll call him when we get back to the house to see if he can speak to us this afternoon."

"We should have another go at talking to the marina employees too," I added. "It really does seem like someone should have seen something."

Kyle tossed the stick into the water once again. Then he took me into his arms and looked me in the eye before kissing me gently on the lips. "See? We're killing this investigation. We have a new suspect list and potential witnesses to interview. We do make a pretty good team, don't we?"

"The best."

"Do you have to be back at the resort at any certain time?"

"I should be home for dinner. I don't want Grandpa or Dad to have to get the girls off to bed. You're invited to come home with me if you want. We could take another walk on the beach after we get the kids to bed."

Kyle leaned in for another kiss just as Pumpkin dropped the wet stick at his feet, then shook water all over both of us. We laughed as we gave in to the fact that the dogs were a lot more interested in playing fetch than in kissing.

"I've been thinking of asking my mom and Annabeth if they wanted to do something fun with Ashley and Gracie this weekend," Kyle said casually.

Kyle's mom lived in Serenity with Annabeth Boswell in a condo he'd bought for her. Kyle and I first met Annabeth when her sister was missing and we'd decided to investigate. It turned out Annabeth's father was one of the bad guys in that particular mystery, and her sister Kiara had become her legal guardian. Kyle had wanted Kiara to be able to attend college, so he'd arranged for Annabeth to live with his mother. She was sixteen now, and Ashley and Gracie both loved hanging out with her.

"Are we thinking of an overnight outing?" I asked.

Kyle glanced at me. "Would you be interested in an overnight outing of some sort?"

I smiled. "Very much. Ashley and Gracie have asked about going to the fair in Sacramento. I don't suppose your mom and Annabeth would be interested in something like that?"

Kyle pulled me into his arms again. "I think they might be very interested in something exactly like that, but I'll ask them."

When we returned to the house, Kyle called his mother, who said she'd be thrilled to spend time with the girls. It occurred to me it would be a good idea for Kyle's mom to spend time with Ashley and Gracie. If Kyle and I were eventually to marry, she'd become their grandmother. Marriage wasn't something Kyle and I had discussed, but even though we'd been taking our relationship frustratingly slow, it had crossed my mind and I was willing to bet he had thought about it as well.

"Mom will pick them up at the resort at eight o'clock on Saturday morning. I reserved a suite near the fairgrounds for Saturday night. Mom said they'd be home around dinnertime on Sunday."

"Sounds to me like we might finally have the night together we've been trying to arrange," I said softly.

"Come hell or high water," Kyle responded before kissing me gently on the mouth.

"Hell or high water," I said and kissed him back.

Kyle groaned and took a step back. "Which brings me to the

next order of business."

"Which is?"

"If you want to look in to Bristow's murder I'm fine with helping out, but whatever happens, Saturday and Sunday are reserved for us. We can work on the case today and tomorrow, but if we haven't figured it out by eight o'clock Saturday morning, we put a pin in it until Monday."

"I totally agree."

"Okay, then. Let's get started. I'll call Conrad. We should have time to meet with him and go out to the marina to talk to some of the employees before we need to head out to the resort."

Doug Conrad was on the town council with Kyle, so they knew each other fairly well. He seemed more than happy to talk with us, so we got the dogs settled and drove over to his insurance office.

"Thank you for meeting with us on such short notice," Kyle said, shaking Doug's hand.

"No problem. Let's use the large table in the conference room. Coffee?"

Kyle and I both declined.

"We wanted to speak to you," Kyle began, "because we understand Striker Bristow was meeting with you at the marina restaurant just prior to him being shot and killed."

"That's correct. He wanted to discuss his mall project, and he brought along his assistant, Gina Roberts."

"I understand Bristow walked you to your car before walking Ms. Roberts to hers," Kyle continued.

"Right. I have to say, even with the concessions Bristow

seemed to be willing to make, I was still on the fence about working with him. His reputation was dicey, to say the least, and while I thought Ms. Roberts did a wonderful job helping him create a marketable plan, I still wasn't sure I wanted to enter into a deal with a man like him. I think Bristow could sense my hesitation because he not only followed me out when I told him I had another appointment to get to, but he followed me to my car, still trying to sell me the entire way. I was happy to finally make my escape."

"When I spoke to Ms. Roberts, she seemed to think the meeting went well," I said.

Doug shrugged. "Bristow is a pushy man who won't take no for an answer. I only agreed to meet with him because he'd been pursuing me relentlessly for weeks. I figured the only way to get him off my back was to give him what he wanted. I suppose I may have appeared to be more interested in the concept than I actually was. Ms. Roberts had prepared a nice presentation and I didn't want to be rude to her. And I knew several council members did want to see the project move forward, so I felt I owed it to them to listen to what Bristow had to offer with at least somewhat of an open mind. Truth be told, however, I couldn't see myself ever signing on to a project with a jerk like him. I have a feeling if he hadn't died, the project would have come to a vote and it would have been shot down despite the chatter around town."

I felt bad for Gina. She'd put in a lot of work and it sounded as if the project had been dead in the water anyway. Of course, she'd already been paid at least part of what was owed to her and she was looking at a whole new start outside of Paradise Lake, so I was pretty sure she wouldn't care one way or the other how things turned out now.

"Bristow was shot just as they arrived at Ms. Roberts's car," Kyle said. "Did you see anything at all that seemed suspicious as you drove out through the parking lot?"

"I was parked close to the restaurant while both Bristow and Ms. Roberts's cars were in the overflow area near the marina. I didn't notice anything as I walked to my car, though I did see there were two men in a blue sedan parked on the street leading away from the lot. I only noticed them because they were parked facing the wrong direction, as if they wanted to make sure to see everyone who left the parking lot."

"It sounds like you saw the men who pursued and kidnapped Gina," I said. "According to her, they weren't interested in Bristow and they didn't shoot him. Did you see anything else? Maybe someone hiding in the bushes or hunched down behind a car?"

Doug shook his head. "I'm sorry. I didn't see anything like that."

"About what time did you leave the restaurant?" Kyle asked.

"I guess it was around seven fifteen."

"Was the parking area still crowded?" Kyle continued.

"The lot nearest the restaurant was packed with the dinner crowd, but the area where Bristow and Ms. Roberts were parked had cleared out quite a lot. Most of the day boaters had come in and left for the day."

"So whoever shot Bristow most likely had a clear shot?" Kyle asked.

Doug nodded. "I would say so. There were maybe ten cars in all still in the marina lot and most were scattered around. Depending on where the gunman hid and the timing of Bristow entering the lot with Ms. Roberts, I could see how a gunman could have shot Bristow and then left without being seen."

"But there were people around who might have seen something?" I asked.

"Sure. There are usually two guys at the boat launch until eight and the marina office is usually open until eight as well. And there were still a few day boaters who hadn't come in yet, or at least they hadn't returned to their cars. The marina closes at eight, but a lot of folks come in from a day on the water and head for the restaurant bar. So I suppose some of the ten or so cars I saw could have belonged to people next door."

The conversation stalled. I glanced at Kyle, who shrugged. I turned back to Doug, not yet ready to give up. "I just have one last question. Do you remember seeing anyone in the restaurant you knew? Maybe someone who came in after you or left just before you did and might have seen something in the parking area?"

"Glen Yorkshire was at the bar when I left. And I remember seeing Stuart Green leave the restaurant just minutes before we did."

"Okay," Kyle said, standing up. "We'll let you get back to work. Thank you again for taking time to meet with us."

"No problem. See you at the next town council meeting?"

"I'll be there," Kyle confirmed.

"I understand choosing a new mayor is going to be on the agenda. I don't suppose you'd be interested?"

"Not at this point," Kyle answered. "It'll be interesting to see who the council comes up with."

After we left Doug's office we headed to the marina and the restaurant to speak to some employees. I was sure Kate and Roy had already done it, but there'd been times in the past when a witness who was unwilling to speak to one of the deputies had been willing to speak to Kyle or me.

"What do you think about the fact that Glen Yorkshire was in the bar the day Bristow was shot?" I asked as we drove.

"I think he just became a much stronger suspect. If he did think his wife was cheating on him with Bristow, he might have been following him around, looking for proof. Maybe he followed him to the restaurant, then left and set up to shoot him while Gina and Bristow were walking Doug to his car."

"That's exactly what I was thinking. Maybe we should try to track him down after we finish at the marina."

"Do you know him?" Kyle asked me.

I frowned. "No, do you?"

"Not at all. I'm not sure if he'll spill much to two strangers asking about the affair his wife was supposedly having and the man he supposedly shot."

"You're probably right. Maybe we should call Roy. He can interview him officially, and that might result in a confession if he did it and now regrets it. I'll call him," I offered.

The parking lot was packed when we arrived at the marina. Kyle found a spot way in the back that appeared to be the last one available. There were people everywhere at this time of the day, so the employees would probably be too busy to speak to us. A quick question that came right to the point would be our best chance of getting a reply.

Both the marina and the restaurant were as crowded as we'd thought they would be. We made a few attempts to get employees to talk to us about the shooting a week before, but except for one waitress, everyone told us they hadn't seen a thing.

"I took my break and went out for a smoke around that time," said the waitress. "The management doesn't want us to smoke nearby, so I went to the back of the parking area, like I always do. There was an old white pickup parked at the very back of the lot. That wasn't that unusual. Boaters who arrive later in the afternoon most likely have to park there, and they're also most likely to be the last to leave. What was odd was that there was a man sitting in the truck. He might have been waiting for someone, and I only had a fifteen-minute break, so I don't know when he got there or how long he stayed."

I knew Byron Wildman had an old Ford truck that I seemed to remember was white. Wildman and Yorkshire would stay firmly at the top of our list.

CHAPTER 17

When we left the marina, I called Roy and filled him in on both the fact that Glen Yorkshire had been seen at the restaurant on the evening Bristow was shot and that he'd told Gina he believed his wife was having an affair with the unpopular developer. I also mentioned that the waitress had seen an old white truck at the scene, and that Kyle and I had seen Wildman working on a truck of the same description. Roy assured me he'd speak to both men.

Kyle knew Stuart Green and he called him, but he didn't pick up. Kyle left a message and we went to his house. It was beginning to get late, so we picked up the dogs and headed back to the resort.

On the way, we discussed our plans for the weekend, which couldn't get here soon enough. At the resort, I filled Ashley in on the plans we'd made for her for the weekend. There was no doubt in my mind Gracie would be thrilled, but Ashley could be tricky. As it turned out, Kristi had plans with her dad anyway, so Ashley was glad to have something fun to do. It looked like Kyle and I might actually have the night together we'd been trying to arrange for over a month. After a difficult summer, I felt like things were finally coming together.

*   *   *

"I have some interesting news," my dad said when the family had finished dinner and Ashley and Gracie had gone into the den to watch a movie. The three of us sat on the deck overlooking the lake as the sky darkened.

"Oh, and what's that?" I asked as I sipped a glass of wine.

"Noah and I were having lunch today when Deputy Baldwin stopped by."

I frowned. "What did she want?"

"She was here to see Noah," Dad informed us. "Apparently, he'd been seen leaving Bristow's office on the afternoon of the day he was shot."

"What? Why would Noah be meeting with Bristow?" I asked, almost spilling my wine in the process.

"Apparently," Dad answered, "Bristow offered Noah a job and he stopped by to speak to him about it."

I narrowed my gaze. "A job? What kind of a job? Noah is a resort manager and Bristow was trying to build a mall."

Dad shifted in his chair. I could see his injury had been bothering him this week. I felt so bad for him, but at least he was walking with only a cane for support. "Bristow wanted to build a mall in Serenity, but he has developments all over the world. From what Noah told me, he owned a large resort in Cancún that he wanted Noah to run."

"He isn't going to?" I asked in a panic. Noah had only been with Maggie's Hideaway for a few months, but he'd really seemed to take ownership of things during Dad's recuperation, and I wasn't sure how we'd manage without him.

Dad shook his head. "Noah told him he had no plans to

leave Maggie's Hideaway. The only reason he agreed to meet with Bristow was because when he first approached him, he made Noah promise to at least think it over rather than making a decision right away. Noah shared that the offer was a good one, but he didn't like to hop between resorts every few months. He prefers to stay in one place for at least a couple of years, and he really loves the employees here and the mountain location."

"So why did Kate want to talk to him?" I wondered.

"I guess because Noah met with Bristow just hours before he died. Noah said he saw him at three o'clock, and Bristow was dead by eight."

"Did Noah know anything?" I asked my dad.

"He said he didn't. He did say a woman Bristow introduced as his wife arrived just before he was leaving."

"That fits with what Mrs. Bristow told Kyle and me. She said she stopped by to see her ex-husband just before four o'clock the day he died. Did Kate say anything else other than ask Noah about his meeting with Bristow?"

"Not to me. Noah walked her out to her car and I noticed the two of them stopped to chat for a good ten minutes before she pulled away. When Noah came back to our table, he jumped right in with a continuation of our conversation about Winter Carnival."

Interesting. I wondered if it might be worth my while to have a chat with Noah. He'd already left for the day, so that would have to wait until tomorrow.

Dad and Rosalie retired to their suite to watch a movie, and Kyle and I headed down to the beach. The crowds had cleared out, so we'd brought a bottle of wine to watch the sunset. There's nothing better than a sunset over Paradise Lake during the long days of summer when the sun sets late and the air is still warm. Kyle arranged the beach chairs we'd brought so they faced the western slope of the mountain while I poured the wine.

"I'm surprised the beach is so deserted," Kyle said. "A week ago there were still plenty of people around at this time of the night."

"I think a lot of schools have already started up. The classes in the valley started this past Monday."

"Seems early."

"It does, but the schools there let out earlier in the spring than we do, so it all works out. Personally, I enjoy this time of the year, when we have the beach to ourselves, yet it's still warm."

"It is nice," Kyle agreed.

We sat in silence for a few minutes, enjoying the setting sun and sipping our wine. After the sun was down we decided to build a fire in one of the pits and finish off the bottle of wine. It was a warm evening, so between the heat from the fire and the sweatshirt I wore, I was toasty warm.

"How do you feel about this thing with Noah?" I asked after a while.

Part of me knew I should be focusing on the romantic atmosphere of the lake and the firelight, but my mind refused to relax. I always did have a hard time doing that when I was investigating a murder, and now was no different.

"I'm not sure. I guess I don't blame Bristow for trying to recruit Noah. He's very good at what he does, and Bristow appeared to me to want the best for himself. Likewise, I'm not surprised Noah chose to stay where he is. Your dad has been very good to him, and the entire family treats him like one of the gang.

"I'd be surprised if Noah knew anything at all about Bristow's murder, but it makes sense that Kate would want to speak to him if he was seen leaving Bristow's office just hours before he was shot."

I laughed. "That pretty well sums it up, but I wasn't asking what you thought but how you *felt*."

"Felt?" Kyle looked confused.

"When Dad initially told us Kate had been by, I was irritated. After he explained why she was here, I found my irritation had evolved into curiosity and anger. If Bristow was trying to poach Noah for one of his other resorts, might there have been others he was trying to poach for one development or another as well?"

"You're thinking Bristow might have been shot by someone negatively affected by his business practices, like trying to recruit the best employees?"

"I know it's another long shot, but at this point I feel like all we can do is grasp at straws. Both Wildman and Yorkshire make good suspects, but we should keep adding to our list in case Roy speaks to them and they both wash out."

"Okay, then other than Maggie's Hideaway, who would have a large enough resort that Bristow might be interested in their management team?" Kyle asked.

"No one on the north shore, but there are a few large resorts on the south shore. At the very least, I think I'll mention it to Roy when I see him next."

Kyle leaned over and took my glass from my hand. "That sounds like a good idea, but for now, what do you say we change the topic from Bristow's murder to our upcoming weekend?"

"Okay. What do you want to discuss?" I asked as Kyle softly touched his lips to mine. I waited for him to respond, but instead, he pulled me onto his lap as he deepened the kiss. As far as I was concerned, Saturday couldn't get here fast enough.

CHAPTER 18

Friday, August 18

I woke the following morning to Gracie crawling into bed with me. It was early, so I opened my arms and she crawled inside and snuggled under the covers. I closed my arms around her and pulled her close to my chest. "Is everything okay?" I whispered into her ear after we'd settled into a comfortable position.

"My head hurts."

I kissed the top of her head, which was tucked under my chin. "I'm sorry, sweetie. It's pretty early still. Do you think you'll be able to go back to sleep?"

She nodded. She rested her head on my chest and I caressed her hair as she drifted off to sleep. Gracie wasn't the sort to have headaches. I hoped she wasn't getting sick.

By the time we woke up, Gracie seemed to be feeling better, although she wasn't quite her usual energetic, happy self. Deciding to err on the side of caution, I suggested she might want to curl up on the sofa in the den with her favorite cartoons rather than going out to the pool with Ashley, as she'd originally planned. I mentioned to both Dad and Grandpa that it seemed like she might be coming down with something and warned them that they might want to stay away from her. I'd planned to work on the murder case with Kyle today, but a potentially sick sister took precedence over everything. The last thing I wanted was for either my dad, who was still on the mend, or my grandpa, who had been dealing with some health issues of his own, to come down with whatever Gracie might have.

After calling Kyle and letting him know I was resort bound for the day, I decided to use my time indoors to work on my lesson plans for the upcoming school year. I couldn't believe the summer break had almost come to an end. It had been a busy and, in many ways, crazy summer. First, I'd broken up with Hunter, who I'd once been certain was the man I was meant to grow old with. Then my dad had become engaged, and I'd decided to spend the summer helping a family friend in South Carolina. We'd just solved the mystery of the body in the attic there and had finally settled down when I'd learned my father had been involved in an accident that had resulted in the death of his good friend Judge Harper. I'd dropped everything and rushed home to be by his side. Since then, I'd shouldered extra duties at the resort to relieve some of the work load created by Dad's absence while he healed. I'd been running nonstop since school let out last spring, but somehow, amid all that insanity, I'd fallen in love with Kyle.

I only hoped Gracie's bug would be short-lived so Kyle and I could finally have the perfect night I'd been dreaming of for weeks. Maybe it was ridiculous in this day and age to want a perfect evening I could remember always, but there was something so special about Kyle that I wanted to be sure all our firsts were special as well.

"Hey, honey. Would you mind doing me a favor?" Dad asked just after I came downstairs after putting Gracie down for a nap.

"Sure. Whatever you need."

"I just got a call from Sterling Snow, asking if I could have someone drop off the preliminary plans we came up with for Winter Carnival. It seems he has a meeting set up with the Florida Ski Council and he's trying to get them to commit to coming to Angel Mountain this year. He thought the Carnival might be just the thing he needed to put his resort in the running."

"I'd be happy to drive the plans up to the resort. I just put Gracie down and she should be fine until I get back. If she does wake up, you need to stay away from her. I don't know what she may have, but whatever it is, I don't want you catching it."

"Rosalie closed the clinic early and is on her way back to the house. If Gracie wakes up before you get back, I'll have her make sure Gracie has whatever she needs."

"Great. I'll just run upstairs and get my bag."

Angel Mountain was the largest ski resort on the north end of the lake. There were several larger ones on the south shore, where most of the population of Paradise County lived and most of the visitors to the area stayed, but Angel Mountain had been working hard to compete with the larger ones. Now it appeared they might just establish the reputation as being a must-ski resort they'd been working so hard for so many years to secure.

It was a clear and sunny day and the trip up the mountain

was beautiful. The higher I climbed in elevation, the more clearly I could see all of Paradise Lake, which from a distance looked to be a sheet of deep blue glass. During the ski season, Angel Mountain was packed with both locals and visitors who made the trip up the mountain for a day on the slopes, but during the summer the parking lots were empty, the ski lifts waited silently, and the lodge, the restaurant, and the ski village were closed.

I parked at the curb near the executive offices and told Echo, who I'd brought along for the ride, to stay. Although it was a warm day down at the lake, it was rather cool up on the mountain. Still, I didn't want Echo, with all his thick black fur, to become overheated, so I made sure I was parked in the shade and rolled all four windows down for air flow. "I'll only be five minutes," I promised my sweet boy before grabbing the plans and heading to the front door of the executive offices.

"My dad asked me to deliver these," I said after making my way through the empty building to Sterling's office and taking the stack of paperwork out of my bag.

"Thanks, just put them on the desk. I'd have come to get them myself, but I've been driving my dad's old truck while mine is being repaired and it decided to be difficult and refuse to start on me."

"Do you need a ride down the mountain?"

"No, I called a tow truck. It should be here soon. If the service can't get the truck started, I'll just have them tow it to the garage in Serenity and catch a ride down the mountain with the tow driver."

I glanced around the office. "Okay, if you're sure. It's so quiet today. I know you're closed, but I expected the management staff to be here. Is it always this dead in the summer?"

Sterling tightened his lips. "No. I normally have a team that works year-round. Unfortunately, it seems I may be faced with hiring a new team this year."

"Everyone?"

"I'm afraid so. My general manager elected to take a job with a competitor and somehow managed to convince my entire management team to make the move with him."

"Wow," I said. "I'm so sorry. I can't imagine having to replace your entire management team. What are you going to do?"

Sterling's face hardened. "I don't know. Angel Mountain has been expanding aggressively for the past couple of years. We have projects that should have been completed by the first snow that have now been put on pause because we don't have the oversight necessary to handle the expansion and take care of the start-up activities required every year." Sterling sighed. "It's really a disaster. I don't know what I'm going to do."

Sterling had a reputation for being a stringent and unyielding man who ruled his ski empire with an iron fist, which didn't engender a lot of loyalty among his employees, but to lose your entire management team all at once...I didn't see how the poor guy was going to recover before the first snow.

I offered my sympathy once again and had turned to go when I noticed a photo on the wall of an older gentleman standing in front of an old stepside truck. A white Ford truck. Suddenly, everything began to fall into place.

"Is that the truck you've been driving?" I asked.

"Yeah. It belongs to my dad."

"Bradford was at the resort the other day looking for my dad. Do you know if he ever got what he needed? I tried to help him, but he didn't want to speak to me."

Sterling's lips tightened. "Dad is supposed to be retired. He gave the resort to me but still he continues to butt in."

"I guess it is hard to totally walk away from something you built with your own hands."

"I know. And I get it. The resort is his first love. He'll die if we lose it, but I don't know if we can get the employees we need in place to open on time. My dad has already had one heart attack. I doubt he'd survive another."

I turned and looked at Sterling, focusing on his face as I made my next statement. "You know, we're a lot alike. We both grew up living at resorts and we both were raised by strong men who built something wonderful with their bare hands."

"I guess that much is true," Sterling said.

"And I do feel your pain about losing your management team. It turns out our general manager was approached as well. With my dad out, it would have been a total catastrophe if we'd lost him," I exaggerated. It would have been rough to lose Noah but not a catastrophe. Still, I wanted Sterling to identify with me, so I played it up.

"What is it about rich businessmen who already have more assets than they can manage but feel the need to poach in another man's pond?"

"It really isn't fair," I agreed. "When my dad told me that Bristow had tried to steal Noah right out from under our noses, I was furious."

Sterling's entire face turned red and he balled his fists. I could see he was trying to suppress his rage. "It might be too late for me, but you don't need to worry about that rodent fishing in your pond. The man has been dealt with once and for all."

I realized it was best to leave then, and let Roy close the case. If I was right—and I was sure I was—Bristow hadn't been shot because of his mall project or the married women he slept with, but because of his lack of business ethics.

I turned to go. "I really should get going."

"Thanks again for bringing up the plans." Sterling picked up the pile of papers I'd placed on the desk. He glanced through them, then pulled one sheet from the bottom. "Seems this got mixed up with the plans for the carnival." Sterling handed it to me. "Are you looking in to Bristow's death?"

Suddenly, I realized the suspect list Kyle and I had come up with had somehow become attached to the Winter Carnival plans. "I was in the beginning, but I've pretty much decided to let the sheriff's department handle it from now on." I took several steps toward the door. "I'll talk to you later."

I walked swiftly through the empty building. The urge to run was strong, but I didn't want Sterling to know I was onto him. I'd just reached the front door when I heard Sterling behind me.

"Tj," he called.

I cringed and stopped walking. I turned around. "Did I forget something?"

"My dad wants to talk to you."

"Bradford's here?"

"Not yet. He heard about the truck and happened to call just after you left my office. I mentioned you were here, and he asked that you wait for him."

"I'd love to catch up with your dad. Really. But my sister is sick, and I need to get back. Maybe we can chat another time." I turned and placed a hand on the door.

"I must insist you wait for Dad as he requested."

It was then I saw the small gun in Sterling's hand. I could wait, and it would be two to one, or I could make a run for it now. Sterling had a gun, but he wasn't all that close to me. All I had to do was shove the door open and run. I took a deep breath and did just that. Once I was clear of the door, I made a sharp turn to the left and ran as fast as I could. I heard Sterling yelling at me. I put my head down and ran faster.

Once I reached the cover of the forest, I thought I'd be home free. I could find a place to hide until it was safe to continue. I ran as hard and fast as I could toward the woods. I felt something brush my hair. A moment later I heard a shot and realized the idiot was actually shooting at me. It was a good thing I liked to jog and stayed in shape. Outrunning bullets fired from a gun was proving to be harder than I'd thought. I'm a fast runner but not faster than a speeding bullet. I dug down deep and sped up just a bit. I saw an area of thick underbrush up ahead and was moving toward it when I found myself flying toward the ground face-first. I landed on my chest and face. Hard. It completely knocked the air from my lungs. I knew I needed to get up, but I was doing good just trying to breath. By the time I finally found my breath, I opened my eyes to find Sterling standing over me, his gun pointed directly at my head.

"Why?" I finally asked.

The muscles in his face contracted to a degree that his appearance was distorted. "I didn't tell you the whole story."

"Which is...?" I sat up very slowly. There was dirt on my

face, in my mouth, and in my eyes, but I knew I needed to make small movements, so I didn't try to brush any of it away.

"Bristow approached my dad about buying Angel Mountain. The resort was my dad's baby, so he refused to sell it. When Bristow realized he wasn't going to get his way, he offered our entire management staff a huge bonus to leave."

He really was a snake! "You can hire more staff. It won't be easy, but there's time before the snow falls."

"No, there isn't nearly enough time. The expansion my dad and I were attempting got the better of us and I'm afraid we ended up deeply in debt to the bank. We missed some payments over the summer and the bank is threatening to foreclose. My dad tried to convince them we'd be able to make up the late payments over ski season, but when the bank manager found out we'd lost our entire management team, he decided to cut his losses and initiated the foreclosure process. Dad's going to lose the thing he loves most in the world because a small man with a Napoleon complex wasn't satisfied ruling his own domain. He needed to rule the world."

I'd been trying to slowly stand when Sterling realized what I was doing. He pointed the gun at my face. "I'm sorry it came to this. Dad has lost the resort, but I'm not going to let him lose his freedom as well."

"Your dad shot Bristow?"

"Isn't that what you already figured out? Isn't that why you ran?"

"Until this moment I thought it was you." My heart began to pound. I'd hoped to talk Sterling into letting me go, but there was no way he was going to do that with his father's freedom at stake.

I closed my eyes and waited for the shot. What I heard instead was a scream. I opened my eyes to find Echo on top of Sterling with the man's arm clenched in his mouth. I got up slowly and approached him. He was screaming at the top of his lungs. What a baby. Echo had a firm grip on him, but he hadn't even drawn blood. I took the gun from the man's hand, then commanded Echo to stand down. He let go of Sterling's arm and took a step back, though he continued to growl. That was fine with me. He'd been planning to kill me. He deserved to feel the terror of having a 130-pound dog standing over him with teeth bared. I took out my phone and called Roy. Talk about a crazy end to a crazy mystery that had almost been the end of me in more ways than one.

CHAPTER 19

Saturday, August 19

It was the night of my big date with Kyle. A night I was sure would be filled with fresh flowers, candles, expensive wine, and romantic music. I'd dreamed of making love with Kyle as the moon shone down on the still lake and through the bedroom window. I'd had so many expectations after building up this night in my head for the past few weeks, I supposed part of me realized I was bound to be disappointed. But as I glanced out the window and saw the moon on the lake just as I'd imagined, I realized that while things hadn't gone *exactly* as planned, this truly was a perfect moment I would hold forever in my heart.

"Despite everything, this is nice," I said as I sat on the bed with a glass of milk while Gracie slept in my lap.

"It is." Kyle smiled back at me.

As it turned out, Gracie had chicken pox. My dad was pretty sure he'd never had them and my grandpa couldn't remember whether he had, so I'd brought Gracie over to Kyle, whose mother had confirmed he'd had them when he was four. Ashley had gone to Sacramento with Kyle's mom as we'd planned, while

Kyle and I played nursemaid to a very sick and very cranky little girl.

"I feel so bad for her," Kyle said as he stroked her hair. "The poor thing is about as miserable as I can remember anyone being."

"She does seem to have a pretty bad case. She should sleep through the night now, though. I followed all of the directions her pediatrician gave me and was assured that once we'd completed all the steps, she'd sleep for at least eight hours."

"I didn't think kids got chicken pox anymore," Kyle said. "Isn't there a vaccine nowadays?"

I nodded. "There is. Apparently, my mom never got around to having Gracie vaccinated, and I guess after she came to live with me I didn't think about it. I still don't have all this mom stuff down."

Kyle leaned over and gently kissed Gracie on the side of the head. She didn't even budge, proving she was out completely.

"Thank you for everything," I said. "Thank you for letting us stay here, and thank you for playing the role of Gracie's maid all day. Thank you for keeping me sane when I wanted to scream in frustration, and thank you for rocking Gracie for hours on end when nothing else would calm her."

"I was happy to help. You know that. I love Gracie. I'll always be here for her."

"Even if she throws up all over your lap again?" I teased.

"Even then."

I couldn't help but smile. Kyle really was one of a kind. He was not only handsome, smart, and caring, but he had the kindest of hearts.

"It's killing me to see her so sick," Kyle said in a soft voice.

"When we have children, let's be sure to remember to get the vaccines."

"Do you think about that?" I asked.

"Vaccines?"

"No, silly. Children. Our children, to be more specific."

Kyle's smile faded just a bit. He lifted the hand that had been stroking Gracie's hair and ran a finger down my cheek. "Will it freak you out completely if I confess that I do think about us having children together?"

I smiled. "Not at all. I think about it too."

Kyle's face lit up. He leaned forward and placed a soft kiss on my lips. When he pulled back, I glanced down at Gracie, who was asleep between us. "I think she's out for the time being. Should we attempt to extricate ourselves from her limbs before it's too late and we're forced to sleep this way? I'm not sure my back can take it."

Kyle nodded. We worked together to carefully lift her limbs so we could move without waking her. Once we were free, we tiptoed out of the room and into the hallway.

"Hang on. I have something for you," Kyle said as he jogged into his bedroom, which was next door to the one occupied by Gracie.

I was half-expecting him to return with flowers or a bottle of wine, but instead he had a bag from the drugstore. He handed it to me. I peeked inside. "A baby monitor?"

"I know you're concerned about Gracie. I am too. I thought if we could keep an ear on her from anywhere in the house, we could head downstairs and try to salvage what's left of our evening."

I almost cried. Lots of men had given me flowers, wine, and

chocolates, but no one had ever given me a baby monitor.

"You know," I said as I handed the monitor back to Kyle, "while a baby monitor is a great idea, maybe we should stay close until we're positive she's asleep."

"Okay, whatever you think is best," Kyle said, although he looked surprised. "I can bring a couple of chairs into her room if you'd like."

I took Kyle's hand in mine. "I don't think that will be necessary. I'm sure she's out for the night, but if she does call out, we should be able to hear her from your room."

Kyle frowned. I could see he was trying to read my face. "Okay. I guess we can lay down for a while. You must be tired after the long day."

I put my arms around Kyle's neck. I pulled his head down to mine and kissed him deeply. "Actually," I whispered against his lips, "I'm not tired in the least."

Kyle's eyes grew big as he began to understand my intent. He raised his hand and used a finger to caress my cheek. "You know I want to be with you more than anything in the world, but I thought you wanted to wait until it was perfect."

I ran my hands down Kyle's back until they settled just below his waist. I looked deeply into his dark blue eyes. "I did and it is."

KATHI DALEY

USA Today bestselling author Kathi Daley lives in beautiful Lake Tahoe with her husband, Ken. When she isn't writing, she likes spending time hiking the miles of desolate trails surrounding her home. She has authored more than seventy-five books in eight series including: Zoe Donovan Cozy Mysteries, Whales and Tails Island Mysteries, Sand and Sea Hawaiian Mysteries, Tj Jensen Paradise Lake Mysteries, Writer's Retreat Southern Seashore Mysteries, Rescue Alaska Paranormal Mysteries, and Seacliff High Teen Mysteries. Find out more about her books at www.kathidaley.com.

The Tj Jensen Mystery Series
by Kathi Daley

Henery Press Mystery Books

And finally, before you go...
Here are a few other mysteries
you might enjoy:

THE AMBITIOUS CARD

John Gaspard

An Eli Marks Mystery (#1)

The life of a magician isn't all kiddie shows and card tricks. Sometimes it's murder. When magician Eli Marks very publicly debunks a famed psychic, said psychic ends up dead. The evidence, including a bloody King of Diamonds playing card (one from Eli's own Ambitious Card routine), directs the police right to Eli.

As more psychics are slain, and more King cards rise to the top, Eli can't escape suspicion. Things get really complicated when romance blooms with a beautiful psychic, and Eli discovers she's the next target for murder, and he's scheduled to die with her. Now Eli must use every trick he knows to keep them both alive and reveal the true killer.

Available at booksellers nationwide and online

Visit www.henerypress.com for details

I SCREAM, YOU SCREAM

Wendy Lyn Watson

A Mystery A-la-mode (#1)

Tallulah Jones's whole world is melting. Her ice cream parlor, Remember the A-la-mode, is struggling, and she's stooped to catering a party for her sleezeball ex-husband Wayne and his arm candy girlfriend Brittany. Worst of all? Her dreamy high school sweetheart shows up on her front porch, swirling up feelings Tally doesn't have time to deal with.

Things go from ugly to plain old awful when Brittany turns up dead and all eyes turn to Tally as the murderer. With the help of her hell-raising cousin Bree, her precocious niece Alice, and her long-lost-super-confusing love Finn, Tally has to dip into the heart of Dalliance, Texas's most scandalous secrets to catch a murderer...before someone puts Tally and her dreams on ice for good.

Available at booksellers nationwide and online

Visit www.henerypress.com for details

BONES TO PICK
Linda Lovely

A Brie Hooker Mystery (#1)

Living on a farm with four hundred goats and a cantankerous carnivore isn't among vegan chef Brie Hooker's list of lifetime ambitions. But she can't walk away from her Aunt Eva, who needs help operating her dairy.

Once she calls her aunt's goat farm home, grisly discoveries offer ample inducements for Brie to employ her entire vocabulary of cheese-and-meat curses. The troubles begin when the farm's pot-bellied pig unearths the skull of Eva's missing husband. The sheriff, kin to the deceased, sets out to pin the murder on Eva. He doesn't reckon on Brie's resolve to prove her aunt's innocence. Death threats, ruinous pedicures, psychic shenanigans, and biker bar fisticuffs won't stop Brie from unmasking the killer, even when romantic befuddlement throws her a curve.

Available at booksellers nationwide and online

Visit www.henerypress.com for details

FATAL BRUSHSTROKE

Sybil Johnson

An Aurora Anderson Mystery (#1)

A dead body in her garden and a homicide detective on her doorstep...Computer programmer and tole-painting enthusiast Aurora (Rory) Anderson doesn't envision finding either when she steps outside to investigate the frenzied yipping coming from her own back yard. After all, she lives in a quiet California beach community where violent crime is rare and murder even rarer.

Suspicion falls on Rory when the body buried in her flowerbed turns out to be someone she knows—her tole-painting teacher, Hester Bouquet. Just two weeks before, Rory attended one of Hester's weekend seminars, an unpleasant experience she vowed never to repeat. As evidence piles up against Rory, she embarks on a quest to identify the killer and clear her name. Can Rory unearth the truth before she encounters her own brush with death?

Available at booksellers nationwide and online

Visit www.henerypress.com for details

Made in the USA
Monee, IL
15 November 2019

16857040R00128